A TINFOIL Sky

Cyndi Sand-Eveland

Tundra Books

Text copyright © 2012 by Cyndi Sand-Eveland

Published in Canada by Tundra Books,
75 Sherbourne Street, Toronto, Ontario M5A 2P9

Published in the United States by Tundra Books of Northern New York,
P.O. Box 1030, Plattsburgh, New York 12901

Library of Congress Control Number: 2011923469

Library and Archives Canada Cataloguing in Publication

Sand-Eveland, Cyndi
A tinfoil sky / by Cyndi Sand-Eveland.

ISBN 978-1-77049-277-6

I. Title.

PS8637.A539T55 2012   JC813.'6 C2011-901450-5

We acknowledge the financial support of the Government of Canada through the Book Publishing Industry
Development Program (BPIDP) and that of the Government of Ontario through the Ontario Media
Development Corporation's Ontario Book Initiative. We further acknowledge the support of the Canada
Council for the Arts and the Ontario Arts Council for our publishing program.

ONTARIO ARTS COUNCIL
CONSEIL DES ARTS DE L'ONTARIO

Design: Jennifer Lum

Printed and bound in the United States of America

This book was produced using recycled materials.

1 2 3 4 5 6   17 16 15 14 13 12

For "Mel," wherever you are.

There was promise in your eyes,
and you left me wanting to write that possibility into existence.

I hope I have done you justice.

Contents

Acknowledgments

Many thanks Kathryn Cole, Kelly Jones, and Kathy Lowinger at Tundra Books for your editorial feedback and encouragement! I am very grateful, Kathryn, that you gave this story not only one chance, but three.

I am deeply indebted to Morty Mint, my agent, and Verna Relkoff and Sharmaine Gray, editors extraordinaire, who read, listened, and offered sage advice.

My dear friends Robyn, Heidi, Val, Anne, daughter Kohe, sisters Sharrie and Jackie, and niece Ashley read and gave feedback on early drafts. Thank you!

Thank you also to Lisa Menna, whose magic and long walks infused the early work on this story.

Philip, Celeste, Sharrie, Sandy, and Mary Ann all willingly shared their experiences and valuable insights. Thank you.

This book has taken time – lots of it – and that has meant that I have, once again, needed the support of my family, Todd, Kohe, and Mclain.

A promise of more time to walk by the river I owe to Patches, our beloved family dog. He, more than anyone, has listened to this story unfold, and his sweet desire to be with me on this journey, whatever the hour I wrote, never wavered.

Ann McDonnell's students at Trafalgar Middle School read my first effort. The afternoon we spent with all of you passionately sharing your opinions, insights, hopes, and dreams for Mel, kept me rewriting. This book is also dedicated to you.

Lastly, but most importantly, I want to thank you, the reader. A story and its characters are nothing more than simple keystrokes inked to a page. It is the reader who breathes life into the characters, allowing them to truly live.

Cyndi

1

Starting Over

"Girl," Cecily said as they sped away from the curb, "we're going home!"

Mel turned and stared at Cecily, not quite believing the word had slipped so easily from her mother's lips.

And the way that Cecily said the word *home* left Mel wondering. Cecily said it like she meant that place you can always go back to, "that" kind of home. Mel knew Cecily wasn't referring to the last place they'd lived. She always called that place The Dive.

And so Mel repeated the word out loud. "Home?"

"I've been thinking it just might be the right time to go back home to Gladys's in Riverview," Cecily said.

Mel sat in a mixture of shock and silence. It was the eleventh time they'd moved in four years. But this time they weren't being evicted, or finding a new place with cheaper rent, or moving in with a friend of Cecily's. This time they weren't just leaving with nowhere to go. They were going to her grandmother's.

Mel didn't remember what Gladys's place looked like, or, for that matter, what Gladys or Tux, her grandfather, looked like. The last time Cecily and Gladys had spoken, Mel was four. She only knew that Tux had died. That was almost nine years ago, and, for as long as Mel could remember, Cecily had refused to tell Mel much about anything that related to her grandparents, the city of Riverview, or the first three years of Mel's life.

As Mel stared out the car window into the dark, vacant streets, she thought about the events of the last hour. She'd woken to Cecily and Craig arguing again. Only this time, it seemed louder and seemed to go on longer than usual. Then the front door slammed – hard. The yelling continued in the street until finally she heard Craig tear out of the driveway on his motorcycle. Cecily had raced back into the house and stormed into Mel's room. Mel had sat straight up in bed. Cecily had grabbed an armload of Mel's clothes from the floor and piled her blanket and pillow on top of Mel's lap, and then she ordered Mel to go and get in the Pinto station wagon.

As Mel stood in the doorway leading into the living room, she looked at the clock that sat on the floor next to the TV. It was 3:39 a.m. She watched as Cecily raced around in a frenzy, gathering her things and stuffing them into a black plastic garbage bag. Mel kept glancing at the front door while Cecily rummaged through Craig's jacket, digging out a pack of cigarettes and some loose change. Then she went into the kitchen and grabbed what was left of a loaf of bread and a jar with the last little bit of peanut butter.

It wasn't until Cecily was trudging out the front door herself, one hand dragging the bag, the other carrying her guitar case, her handbag clenched between her teeth, that she noticed Mel.

Letting her handbag fall to the floor, Cecily yelled, "I told you to get in the car! Now!"

Mel ran. And, as she ran, she had to keep gathering up the unruly heap of clothes, blanket, and pillow that seemed determined to fall from her grasp.

She was glad to be leaving Craig's place. They'd only been living with him for two months, but it was the worst two months Mel could remember.

They hadn't driven more than ten blocks and were just pulling onto the highway when Mel realized that her journal and small collection of books were still in her room.

"We need to go back!" Mel shouted.

Cecily gave Mel a quick look as she merged the Pinto into traffic. "Can't do that, kiddo," she said.

"No, you don't understand. My books and my . . ."

"Listen, Mel," Cecily said without taking her eyes off

the road. "We can't. Craig is probably back at the house by now."

Both the book set and the journal had been a gift from Cecily for Mel's twelfth birthday. It was one of the few times Cecily had been able to afford to get Mel the gift that she had wanted. It had felt too good to be true. In the weeks since her birthday, she'd read all of the books except one, *The Last Battle*, the final book in the series. She'd been saving it.

What Mel also knew was that with the pillow and blanket now off of her bed, anyone walking into the room would see the outline of her journal under the sheet that covered the mattress. What Cecily didn't know was that the journal had become a place for Mel to express things she couldn't say to anyone else.

"I'm doing this for you, Mel," Cecily said, interrupting Mel's thoughts.

Mel turned around and leaned over the front seat to pull her blanket and pillow out of the heap of clothes that were strewn across the back.

Cecily found a song she liked on the radio, and began belting out the words as though she was singing live for a thousand people.

The thought of Craig finding her journal left Mel feeling weak.

2

Dreaming

Cecily continued to drive through the night with the hope of reaching Riverview by the next afternoon. Mel tried to sleep, but much of the drive was spent in and out of a series of nightmarish dreams.

In the first dream, Craig ripped her bedroom apart. He'd found her journal. He was reading aloud the words she'd written. "I hate him. I hate everything about him."

Then he saw her standing in the doorway. He sneered.

Mel tried to run. Her feet stuck to the floor. She tried to scream – nothing.

She woke up to find herself in the car, with Cecily's hand stroking her hair. She cuddled up to Cecily, who instinctively put one arm around her as she continued to drive.

Mel quickly fell back to sleep, maybe for a minute or maybe an hour, but Craig was back again. This time he was ripping out the page about the police, about Mel's plan to call the police and tell them that Craig was dealing drugs. As Craig ripped the pages, Mel's dream took a turn. It left the scene of Craig and Mel, and it turned to Cecily, Craig, and the police.

The police had Cecily.

Mel was pleading with the them to let her go, but the police weren't listening. They were leaving. Cecily was in the car. Craig wouldn't let Mel run after her.

And it had felt so real – too real. When she woke up this time, the car was stopped on the side of the road. Cecily was holding her.

"Do you want to talk about your dream?" Cecily asked.

"No. But do you think Craig will come looking for his car?"

"This car is half mine," Cecily said as she looked back over her shoulder. "So don't worry. And I've already put three hours between him and us."

Cecily pulled the car a little farther off the highway and made space in the back for the two of them. With Cecily close, Mel felt safe, and the nightmarish dreams felt far away. She couldn't help but hope that this time things were really going to work out. They both slept until morning, when the sun made the car too hot for sleeping.

3

A Trick to Remember

It seemed to take forever to reach Riverview. And the expectation of seeing Gladys, who Mel hadn't seen in almost a decade and couldn't remember, left her feeling anxious. The rate at which Cecily was finishing one menthol cigarette and then lighting another increased until she was chain smoking, lighting the next cigarette from the last one before she butted it out.

Mel read the sign out loud as they crossed the city limits. "Welcome to Riverview, Home of the Wildcats. Population: Forty-five thousand five hundred."

"Here goes nothing," Cecily said.

"Gladys knows we're coming, right?" Mel asked.

"Uh, well, not exactly. I was going to call once we were on the road, but, well . . . there's no point calling now."

The plan was starting to feel like another one of Cecily's failed great ideas.

As they drove through the newer subdivisions, Mel tried to imagine exactly what "home" was going to look like. Before long, they were in an older neighborhood, with big trees and narrow streets.

"Four more blocks," Cecily said, as though she was counting them down. "One left turn, then a right, and we'll see Frohberger's, and then one more block and we're home."

Mel noted that it was the third time Cecily had used the word *home*.

"Frohberger's?" Mel asked.

"Yeah, the corner store. Mr. Frohberger was your grandpa Tux's best friend. It was the two of them that came up with the idea to do the Saturday Magic Matinees in the back of Frohberger's store."

"Did I ever go to the shows?" Mel asked.

"No, it was back when I was a kid. But you know the coin trick where I pull a quarter out from behind your ear?"

Mel nodded. She was enjoying this rare event. Cecily was talking about the past and about their life with Gladys and Tux.

"Well, Tux used to do that trick for you with a bouquet of bright, orange plastic flowers."

"That's funny," Mel said.

"He was funny; I'm amazed you don't remember him."

"I wish I did," Mel said as she looked out the window. It seemed to her that if there had ever been a time to ask the question, the time was now. "So did I live with Gladys and Tux for a long time?"

"No, just sort of off and on. It's not like you lived with them all the time or anything." Then Cecily added, "They were just helping me out through some tough times." She paused. "If I'd known that Tux was sick, I wouldn't have left."

Mel didn't know what to say.

"I wonder if Mr. Frohberger is still alive . . ." Cecily said more to herself than to Mel. "I probably owe him an apology also."

It was something Mel liked about Cecily: that even though Cecily made mistakes, and she made a lot of them, she would apologize.

4

Gladys's

Cecily pulled the Pinto up to the curb and stopped. "Here we are."

"Wow, it's huge," Mel said, gazing up at the three-storey building.

"Oh, don't get your hopes up; Gladys's apartment is right there," Cecily said as she pointed up to the second floor. "You see those two windows?"

"The windows that have the tinfoil on them?" Mel asked.

"Ah, yeah. I don't remember the tinfoil. But anyway, the one on the right, that's the kitchen window and there are two bedrooms and a bathroom off the kitchen. The bathroom is by far the best part of the apartment. The window on the left is part of the living-room-slash-entry. The bigger window next to that is the hallway to Gladys's front door."

Mel noted that it was the only one of the three that didn't have tinfoil. "Are you sure Gladys still lives here?"

Mel asked, sizing up the neighborhood. "Maybe she moved, or maybe she's at work . . ." Mel said quietly, thinking of all the possible reasons Gladys wouldn't be there.

"Probably not at work," Cecily answered as she leaned out the window and looked up at the apartment building. "It's after two in the afternoon, and I suspect she's still working at Fan's Dry-Cleaning – she starts work at six-thirty and is home by two, one-thirty on short days."

"Really, do you think she's still doing the same job?" Mel asked.

"I don't know what else she'd do," Cecily said as she got out of the car. She leaned down and butted out her cigarette on the sidewalk, and then tucked the remaining bit back into the tinfoil pouch inside the package. "The place is looking a little rougher than I remember," she said.

Mel wondered why they had waited so long to come home. Why was it Cecily refused to talk about Gladys and Tux? What had suddenly changed? She was definitely curious, but she didn't ask. This was the closest they'd ever come to going home, and she wasn't going to do anything to stop it from happening. She hoped that being here would spark her memory of the first three years of her life.

The building's exterior wasn't as nice as she'd imag-ined it would be, but nor were any of the other similar buildings that lined both sides of the street. Most had peeling paint, and the gardens were overgrown with weeds; some buildings had broken windows fixed with tape and cardboard.

As they walked along the sidewalk to the front door, Mel was careful not to step on any cracks in the concrete. It wasn't easy: there were tons, and they were all connecting and interconnecting. One line of a nursery rhyme repeated itself in her head as she tiptoed. *Step on a crack; break your mother's back.* Cecily paid no attention to the thin crevices. Mel wished she would.

There was an intercom on the wall outside of the door, and a list of names that had been punched out of blue plastic – the kind done with a labeling machine. Many of the small, gray buttons didn't have name tags. Cecily didn't push the button next to the name Tulley; rather, she pulled on the door and it opened.

"This thing hasn't worked for years," Cecily said as she looked back at Mel and proceeded up the staircase. At the top, the hallway went in two opposite directions. Cecily turned left. They walked four steps and then made a right and continued down the hallway. Gladys's apartment was at the end, next to the window Cecily had pointed out from the Pinto.

Mel followed, looking for anything that might seem

familiar about the rough plaster walls or high ceilings. She had decided on the way to Riverview that she would call her grandmother Grandma, the proper name for a grandparent (and not Gladys, the name Cecily used). With each step, she recommitted to that idea.

5

Knock, Knock

"You knock," Cecily said as she backed away from the door.

Mel took in a deep breath, stepped forward, and knocked. The sounds of a TV filtered through the varnished wooden door.

"Louder," Cecily whispered.

Mel knocked again, this time striking the door with enough force to make her knuckles hurt, but the pain only fueled her excitement. Someone lowered the volume on the TV. Cecily motioned for Mel to knock again. Mel's heart began to pound.

"Who's there?" a woman called out from behind the closed door.

"Is that you, Gladys?" Cecily asked.

Standing purposely tall and perfectly still, Mel held her breath and kept her hands at her sides.

When Gladys didn't answer, Cecily spoke again. "It's Cecily," she said as she gave Mel a nervous smile and a little poke with her elbow. "Say hi," she whispered.

Mel took in a small breath, and, on the exhale, whispered, "Hi."

Still nothing.

Mel could still feel her heart beating against the inside of her chest, but the excitement had turned to nervous dread. She looked out the window; she could see the top of the Pinto parked out front.

"Gladys!" Cecily called out. And then, in an even louder tone, added, "It's Cecily and Melody! We've . . ." Cecily paused. "We've come for a visit."

"Go away!" Gladys shouted back. "There isn't anything left in here for you to steal!"

Cecily seemed to ignore Gladys's statement. "Look!" she said as she pulled Mel in front of her and stared directly at the small brass peephole in the door. "I've got Melody – you know, your granddaughter."

"Let's go," Mel said, undoing herself from Cecily's grasp.

"Gladys! Open . . . the . . . door!" Cecily yelled.

She waited a moment, but there was no response.

"I was hoping," Cecily said in a much calmer voice, "that Mel and I might be able to stay, maybe a day or two, while we looked for a place of our own."

A place of our own, Mel repeated in her head. *I thought*

we were coming here to be home. "I'm trying to get back on my feet." Cecily quickly glanced at Mel and then continued, "No drugs, no booze."

Still, there was no response from Gladys.

"Look, I can understand you not wanting to see me, but what about Melody? What'd she ever do to you?"

Mel could taste the rage building in Cecily's words. "Let's leave," she pleaded.

Cecily ignored her and began pounding on the door with both fists. In this way, Mel and Cecily were different; when things went wrong, which they inevitably did, it was Mel who needed to stay calm and think things through with hopes of counterbalancing the anger in Cecily's quick temper. But in many other ways, they were the same: thin and fine-boned, agile with long, slender hands. Cecily wore her hair in long, straight braids, unlike Mel's tight-knit, copper-colored curls. Her curls were the one thing, she believed, that she got from her father – whoever he was.

"That's it," Gladys yelled. "I'm calling the cops!"

Mel heard what sounded like a chair or table being pushed up against the door. Moments later, the volume on the TV was turned up another notch or two.

"The grand total of all that crap in your jewelry box . . . thirty-five bucks, Gladys!" The TV volume cranked again and was now so high that Mel was sure that Gladys wouldn't hear her no matter how loud Cecily yelled or pounded on the door.

"That's it! Thirty-five bucks! You act like I pawned the queen's jewels or something!" As Cecily yelled, she reached into her coat pocket, pulled out the last of the little money they had left, threw it, and then kicked the door. "There, I hope this makes you happy!"

Two fives and a ten lay on the floor.

"You heard her," a young guy said, poking his head out from his apartment door down the hall. "She said to leave her alone or she's calling the cops."

"Shut up!" Cecily yelled back at him.

"And if *she* doesn't," the guy added, "I will!"

"I'm going to the car," Mel said, and then she turned and began to walk down the hall. As her feet descended the staircase, she could feel a rubbery looseness in her knees. She let everything she'd hoped this day would bring tumble down the dusty and scuffed wooden treads of the stairs. What remained was a cold, empty hole in her stomach.

Cecily continued yelling at Gladys as she stomped down the stairs behind Mel, and she continued yelling all the way out the front door. Then she stood on the parched remnant of a lawn, two floors down from

Gladys's apartment, and yelled up at the closed window.

Mel got into the Pinto and prayed to a god she didn't really know. *Please make Cecily stop, get in the car, and drive away.*

"I should have known it wouldn't work," Cecily yelled half in Mel's direction and half at the apartment building. "We're better off on the street."

Mel couldn't believe what she was hearing. The street was where they had been before moving in with Craig. They'd slept in shelters, they'd sung for handouts, and panhandled on street corners. *How could we be better off on the street?*

"If Tux were alive, he would never have done this, Gladys!" Cecily shouted as she shook her fist in the direction of the window. "He wouldn't have turned away his own *flesh* and *blood!*"

Cecily took her cigarettes out of her bag, lit the half-smoked butt, and blew a steady stream of smoke in the direction of the window as though waiting for Gladys to yell back. When there was no response, Cecily turned and marched to the car.

Cecily no sooner started the car than she shut it off, jumped out, and ran back into the apartment building. Mel turned her head purposely away and looked in the direction of Frohberger's. The store, with its fresh, grassy-green paint and cream trim, was the best-kept building on the entire street. It was the image, in many ways, that she'd held in her heart of what Gladys's was going to look like.

When Cecily returned a few minutes later, she looked exuberant. "Got there just in time. That'll teach her for not opening the door," she exclaimed as she held up the cash, started the engine, and sped away.

For Mel, there was no exuberance because she knew now that they were definitely *not* going home.

They drove for what seemed like hours, traveling up one side of the main street and back down the other, five maybe six times, then along the river, through other neighborhoods, and then back into the downtown. Cecily played tour guide, nostalgically pointing out the bars and restaurants of her old hometown, but it was obvious to Mel that Cecily was looking for someone she knew. They returned time and time again to a public phone booth, where Cecily made several calls but got no answer.

"And look, Mel," Cecily said as she gave Mel a little jab. "They have a library – four floors of books, a pretty nice place for a town this size."

Mel didn't look. Nor did she say anything; instead, she continued to lean her head against the edge of the open window and watch as the streetlights flickered on above the Mission Soup Kitchen. The thought of the library only reminded her that Craig had probably gone back to the house, and that he'd probably found her journal.

She looked into the shops and houses they drove by. Warm light glowed through softly colored curtains. She could almost smell the sweet aroma of summer barbecues, but it only added to the doubt that anything so good could ever be hers. There were no words for the feelings lost inside of her, just emptiness.

Cecily drove them to the edge of town, and then she slowed the car to peer into the darkness for a campground sign. Suddenly a distinct hissing noise, one that appeared to be coming from under the dash, brought Mel's eyes back into the car; a caution light was blinking. She was about to point it out to Cecily when smoke began billowing into the air from somewhere under the hood.

Cecily pulled the Pinto wagon to the edge of the road and began a tirade. She got out, kicked the tires, lifted the hood, and slammed it back down. It wasn't the first time water had come spewing out from the radiator and bubbled over onto the engine. What was different this time was the goop leaking out the bottom onto the road.

Cars drove by – some slowed. Mel hoped someone

would stop. But that was unlikely, especially with Cecily yelling at the car.

When Cecily calmed down, Mel asked, "What are we going to do?"

"I don't know," Cecily answered. "But for now, we need to get this piece of junk off the road." Mel steered while Cecily pushed the car over a grassy area onto a patch of old asphalt, which was next to a pillar under an overpass that was, for the most part, out of view of passing cars. With the Pinto parked, they dug out their clothes and draped them like curtains over the car windows. Mel lit Cecily's cigarette lighter and held up the flame so Cecily could find the bag of bread in the back. Cecily tore each of the two remaining pieces in half, undid the lid on the peanut butter, and scraped what was left from the edge of the jar with the bread, making them each a sandwich.

With the clothes draped over all the windows, the car felt like one of the many childhood forts Mel remembered building.

"Would you like some tea and cake?" Mel asked, holding up a pretend teapot in one hand and the peanut butter sandwich in the palm of the other.

"Oh, that would be nice," Cecily said, holding out her pretend cup and then sipping the hot pretend tea.

They both sat in the back of the car, drinking their tea and eating their cakes.

When Cecily finished hers, she put her hand on Mel's knee. "I'm really sorry about what happened at Gladys's today," she said. "I just kind of lost it."

"It's okay," Mel said, lowering the pretend teapot. Cecily lit her last cigarette of the night, and then, when Mel was finished her sandwich, curled up beside Mel.

It was difficult to get comfortable. In the place where the backseat folded down, there was an edge that dug into Mel's hip. Each time, when she seemed to be finally nodding off, the words "Go away!" stabbed the place in her heart that had been dreaming about going home.

6

July 7

When they woke up, Cecily announced that they should stay on in the broken-down Pinto until they could figure out some way to get it fixed. They got out of the car and took a good look at everything they hadn't been able to see last night in the dark.

"This little spot," Cecily said as she walked through the tall grass, "is not only better than any old campsite, it's free! I mean, look at that! Riverfront camping."

It isn't much of a river, Mel thought. *It's more like a creek.* But the edge was blanketed with tiny, smooth, and creamy white-colored pebbles – perfect for walking barefoot.

But first things first," she added. "We need to get some breakfast!"

Cecily remembered a bakery that made what she called incredible delicacies. And with that thought in mind, they organized themselves and made the ten-minute walk into town.

Everything about the little bakery, from its paned glass windows to the overflowing flower boxes of nasturtiums to a bright cobalt blue bench, felt welcoming.

Mel loved the smell of the fresh bread, and, as she breathed it in, she gazed at the array of scrumptious baked goods. Spending their last few dollars on a treat was something that came easily to Cecily. She'd often say, "Let's go for it. It might be awhile before we've got money to do this again." And so here they stood, mouths watering before a world of wonderful sweets.

"Pick one," Cecily said, encouraging Mel. "Whatever you want."

"Are you sure?"

"Come on," Cecily repeated. "Pick whatever you want."

Mel chose a blueberry muffin. Cecily chose a chocolate-filled croissant. "And one of each to go also," she told the cashier as she handed her a ten dollar bill.

Next door to the bakery was a little market. Cecily went in and bought a jug of milk and a pack of smokes. Mel did the math. Two blueberry muffins cost three dollars, two chocolate croissants cost three or four, one jug of milk costs about two, and cigarettes cost seven dollars. That meant that fifteen or sixteen of their last twenty-some dollars were gone.

—

They passed the milk back and forth between them as they walked back to the Pinto. Once there, Mel pulled her blanket out of the backseat, walked to the river's edge, and laid the blanket down in the tall grass. Cecily followed her.

"Let's make a list," Cecily said, "of all the different kinds of muffins we'll make when we get our next place."

It was a game Cecily played often: The List Game. It wasn't like anything on the list ever got done or happened. When Mel was little, it always cheered her up – but not anymore. Now Mel saw it as dreaming – silly, stupid dreaming.

"It'll be fun," Cecily said, encouraging Mel.

"I don't really want to."

"What do you mean? You love this game."

"Maybe when I was a kid, but not anymore."

Cecily ignored Mel's apparent disinterest and changed the subject. "Do you remember when you wanted to change your name to Strawberry Blueberry Raspberry?" Cicely asked.

"I was six. Kids say things like that when they're six," Mel said as she stared up into the clear blue sky.

What Mel really wanted to talk about was what they were going to do now. If it was true that the twenty dollars

Cecily threw on the hallway floor outside of Gladys's was the last money they had, then that meant they were almost broke. Even if they wanted to, there wasn't enough money to buy the gas to get back to the city. Gladys had been their only option, and although Mel didn't say it out loud, she was mad at Cecily for whatever it was that she'd stolen from Gladys.

She was about to ask Cecily if there was anyone else she knew in Riverview that could help them out when they heard a vehicle pull up somewhere in the direction of the Pinto. Doors opened. There were two voices.

Cecily and Mel pasted themselves to the blanket, hardly breathing, hoping the tall grass concealed their presence. Moments later, doors closed. An engine started, followed only by the sound of tires rolling over the loose stones on the worn pavement. They both sat up.

"We need to figure out a way to get this car fixed and get out of here," Cecily said as she lowered her head to the blanket.

Mel got up and walked over to the car. What caught her eye first was the large fluorescent-pink sticker stuck to the driver's side window.

The date July 7 was written in black felt marker. They had two days. The Pinto needed to be moved or it was going to be towed. Mel walked back to the blanket and broke the news to Cecily.

"This is a free country and if I want to park under an overpass for a week or two, no one is going to tell me I can't." Cecily said it as though this was a matter she had a choice in. Mel didn't bother to disagree; instead, she walked back to the Pinto, opened the door, and began folding and sorting the mess of clothes.

7

Looking for a Gig

The next morning, Cecily woke up with a plan in her head. She was going to look for work. Bars and restaurants often hire singers or musicians to perform for their patrons. One, maybe two nights worth of singing and they'd be able to get the car on the road.

"I might even be able to get a regular gig," Cecily said.

Mel didn't like the thought of Cecily being out at night, but tips were better in a bar or at a fancy restaurant than on the street.

The same scene played out in bar after bar all morning. Cecily would go inside, guitar in hand, and ask to speak to the manager. Mel would find a patch of shade, if there was one, and wait. Sometimes she would hear Cecily singing and Mel would cross her fingers. But no one, it seemed, was hiring.

Cecily decided to give up for the morning and suggested they get some lunch at the Mission Soup Kitchen.

It would give them a chance to sit down, she told Mel, and get out of the blistering sun. The line for food was long; she and Cecily leaned against the building in an effort to squeeze out a little bit of shade. Mel glanced up at the library window; her eyes caught those of a boy, about her age, looking down in her direction. Mel untied her sweatshirt from around her waist, put it on, and pulled the hood onto her head to avoid being seen.

When they finally got inside, Mel noted that the soup kitchen was not all that different from others they had eaten at. It was a large, plain room. Tables were arranged in two rows; there was an aisle down the middle, and at the back stood two worn and weathered brown couches. Cecily went up to the serving window to get their lunches and Mel found them a place at a table. The room's only art (and Mel wasn't sure you could really call it *art*) was a message: the words "Jesus Lives Here" painted in large pastel letters above the counter. As people shuffled past the table, Mel noticed the cooks, who greeted each person as they loaded plates. It seemed that the cooks knew many of the people by name. But Mel was tired, and it was soon easier to close her eyes and rest her head on the table than to take in more of the hustle and bustle of the soup kitchen.

—

"Is she feeling okay?"

Mel awoke to a warm, heavy hand resting on her forehead. She looked up. An absolutely enormous woman with a colorful chili-pepper apron towered over her.

"She's fine," Cecily said, "just tired."

Mel smiled at the woman. She was one of the women she'd spotted in the kitchen serving the lunch. "I'm fine," Mel said.

The cook, or whoever she was, smiled and walked back through the swinging metal door and into the kitchen.

The dark burgundy soup was both sweet and tangy. Mel carefully spooned bits of the dollop of sour cream into each mouthful of beets and cabbage. She wanted to savor the creamy texture, but Cecily was in a rush, and as soon as Mel finished they were back on the move.

The afternoon was no different than the morning. Only now Mel was *really* tired. Cecily began asking about work anywhere: fancy shops, shoe stores, grocery stores, and offices. *It was as though*, Mel thought, *Cecily was proving to herself there was no work, no hope of fixing the car, no hope of finding a place, no hope of anything.*

Finally Cecily stopped and lit a cigarette.

"Your turn," she said to Mel as she slumped down on the sidewalk.

Mel coiled her purple scarf into a small basket, stood tall, closed her eyes, and began to sing. Sometimes she sang country, and sometimes she sang the blues. But today, maybe because she and Cecily were in need of a prayer, she sang gospel.

People stopped, some of them shadowing the sun that shone on her face. Quarter after dime after nickel after quarter fell onto her scarf basket. Two hours passed, her throat was raw, but she'd made twenty-six dollars.

"Do you think we've got enough to get the car fixed?" Mel asked.

"Maybe."

Mel noticed an odd, but familiar look on Cecily's face, as though Cecily was hiding something.

"I can keep singing," Mel offered.

"No, we're good."

"We are still planning to get the car fixed, right?" Mel asked.

Cecily didn't answer right away, and so Mel inquired further. "Or are you thinking of paying Gladys back for the stuff in the jewelry box?"

"Are you kidding?" Cecily said as she got up. "Look, I'm bagged. Let's grab some chips, go back to the Pinto, and call it a night."

—

The next day, as they approached the soup kitchen, Mel looked up at the library window again. The teenage boy that had been peering down at the line yesterday wasn't there today. Mel was relieved.

She and Cecily were about to go inside to eat when Cecily told Mel to go in on her own and to save her a place, that she'd be right back. Mel figured Cecily was going for another smoke, but she'd also noticed that Cecily had been acting just a little bit strange all morning. Mel went in and waited, hungrily. After a few minutes, she went and picked up her lunch and sat down at the table by herself. She set her thin purple scarf on the bench beside her, saving a spot for Cecily. Ten minutes passed. Then fifteen, then twenty. No Cecily.

Where are you? The thought grew louder in Mel's head with each passing minute. Mel pushed her mashed potatoes back and forth across her plate. Every time the door opened, she looked over; every time she heard footsteps, she turned in their direction. No Cecily. Before long, it was just Mel, a small black cat sleeping on the window ledge, and a guy asleep on one of the two brown couches.

When the same woman who'd touched her forehead the day before came out of the kitchen carrying two pieces of cake, Mel wondered if she was going to be asked to leave. Instead, the woman pulled a chair up to the end of the table and sat down.

"And so, what would be the name God gave you?" the cook asked.

Mel almost laughed. "My name's Melody, but I go by Mel."

"Well, it's a pleasure to meet you, Mel."

"My name's Rosemary. My friends call me Rose."

"Nice to meet you," Mel replied.

"I sure hope you like the corner cuts on cake," Rose said as she slid the piece of chocolate cake in front of Mel. It had icing on the top and two sides.

"Oh, that's okay. I'm not hungry," Mel said. Something brushed up against her leg and she looked down to the floor.

"Are you waiting for your friend?" Rose asked.

"She's not my friend; she's my mom," Mel replied and looked again in the direction of the door. She then reached down to pet what she could now see was the black kitten. It was odd to use the word *mom*; Cecily preferred Mel to call her by her name.

"Well, you're welcome to enjoy this piece of cake while you wait," Rose said, and she handed Mel a spoon.

Cecily's blatant absence made Mel nervous, but the cake did look good.

"Would you like some ice cream with that?" Rose asked.

"Sure," Mel answered, suddenly happy for the company. The kitten continued to rub its face and body against Mel's leg.

"Gus!" Rose called out in the direction of the kitchen. "This here young woman would like her pie à la mode!"

Mel loved the way Rose's deep bass voice dragged out the O sound in *mode*. Minutes later, the fellow named Gus – who had, in fact, served her lunch – appeared from behind the metal door, carrying a plastic tub of ice cream and a scoop.

"One scoop or two?" he asked, showing her his toothless grin.

"One's good, thanks," Mel said.

Mel could feel Rose silently studying her. She hoped Cecily would show up soon.

"My mom will be here right away," she said, answering the question she was sure Rose was thinking.

"That's fine," Rose said. "We're here for awhile longer anyway."

The little black kitten found its way onto Mel's lap, popped its head up, and peered over the table. It made Mel laugh.

"We call him Fearless," Rose said. "Kitchen cat by

day, street cat by night. He just showed up here one day, about a week ago, looking for a home."

Mel scooped a bit of the ice cream onto her finger and let Fearless lick it off. She had always wanted a cat, but it had never worked out – even though Cecily had often promised that she could have one.

When Cecily still hadn't arrived fifteen minutes later, Mel swept the few crumbs that had fallen to the table into her hand, brushed them off onto her plate, and then stood up to leave.

"Thanks for the soup and sandwich. And the cake." Mel gave a nervous laugh and added, "And the ice cream. It was all really good."

"Wouldn't feed anybody anything that I wouldn't feed my own family," Rose said, pushing her hands down onto the tabletop and rising up from her chair.

Mel smiled at Rose, gave Fearless another pet, and then walked out through the door.

She stood for a few moments, looking in one direction and then the next. A few of the people who'd also eaten at the soup kitchen were lingering in small groups outside.

"You looking for someone?" a young guy asked.

"No," Mel answered and immediately turned and

began to walk in the direction of the river and the Pinto.

She jumped when Cecily called out her name as she passed the side of the soup kitchen building.

"Man, I thought you'd never come out of there," Cecily said.

"Where were you?" Mel asked.

"Right here," Cecily said.

Her arms hung at her sides, and smoke circled up from one hand. Her head rolled as though it was loose on her shoulders. "Been waiting right here."

It was the way Cecily said the word *right* that gave her away, and, as Mel stepped closer, the smell of booze on Cecily's breath told her the rest. Cecily picked up her purse from the asphalt, threw her arm around Mel's shoulders, the way she often did when she drank, and they staggered back to the Pinto. It wasn't the time to talk about the money.

From the back of the car, Mel watched as Cecily sat outside, propped up against the concrete pillar, drowning her anger in the contents of a bottle of cheap red wine. With each swig, Cecily talked louder, engaged in a one-sided argument. Mel listened as Cecily's words gained force – and then *smash!* The glass bottle hit the concrete, pieces flying in every direction. Mel got out of the car and walked over to Cecily, who was now half-lying against the concrete pillar, and helped her to the car. Cecily started to mumble about Tux. How Tux would never have turned them away. How Gladys had never forgiven her for any mistake she'd ever made.

One day fell into another. And another. After the first week, Mel quit worrying about the car being towed. It seemed that the date on the sticker, the one that Cecily had long since removed, had been more of a scare tactic than a real threat.

Mel also quit going into town with her mother. Cecily had become reckless, especially with the shoplifting, and she had been caught three or four times in different stores. Mel remembered the shame of being told they could never come into a store again – or worse. Cecily didn't object when Mel told her that she'd rather go to the library or stay at the Pinto than go into town with her.

So they came up with a plan. The key to the Pinto was to be left on the front tire by the driver's side, under the frame. This way, whoever came back first had a safe place to wait. In particular, it was for Mel. Cecily was rarely home until late.

Most mornings Mel went to the library, and most days the teenage boy she'd seen peering from the library window could be found reclining on a couch or chair somewhere. Mel came up with a little game of predicting what section she might see him in. He was almost always asleep, and so she gave him the nickname Sleeping Beauty. Once she'd found him, she made a point of *not* walking directly past him.

Instead, Mel walked up and down the long aisles as though she was selecting books to take home. It reminded her of her favorite years, when things had been pretty good. Cecily hadn't been drinking and had a job waiting tables in a café – and she always managed to bring something home from the café for Mel's lunch. On Friday nights, Cecily would take Mel to the library and they'd check out a movie. And even though there had never been quite enough money, the library had been a place where Mel felt rich. That had been one of the few times Mel remembered when she had begun and finished a school year in the same class.

Cecily had always chosen books filled with pictures of interesting and beautiful places. Mel loved to curl up in a chair with her and they'd dream about visiting them all. Cecily told her they just needed a lucky break. "It'll happen, Mel," she often said. "One day we'll be singing *all* over the world; we'll be famous."

Mel also went to the Mission Soup Kitchen every

day for lunch. It was her only real meal of the day. But now she approached the soup kitchen from the opposite direction and waited until everyone else went in. She'd quickly glance up at the library window to make sure Sleeping Beauty wasn't watching, and then slip into the mission.

Sometimes Rose peeked her head into the dining room, found Mel in the crowd, nodded, and went back into the kitchen. Always, Fearless left his spot on the window ledge and pranced over to Mel and curled up on her lap. If Mel was on her own, Rose packed up a to-go container for Cecily. Some days, Rose sat down at the table with her. She didn't ask questions. Mel liked that. Most days, Mel ate and left before everyone else had returned to the street.

If Cecily wasn't outside the soup kitchen when Mel came out, which happened more often than not, Mel walked back to the Pinto, but not before stopping to sing on the corner of Olive and Fifth. There she could be assured of making at least five dollars, sometimes fifteen, in an hour. And she'd noticed that some people were becoming regulars – they didn't just give her money; often they would compliment her singing or ask how her day was going. But there was one creepy guy; he would go by three or four times. The first time, Mel took his money.

But when he showed up again minutes later, she'd figured him out, and she made a point of always looking in another direction.

She didn't tell Cecily about the singing, or the money. Instead, she hid the cash under the front passenger seat floor mat. When the time was right, and there was enough money, Mel would tell her. They'd get the car fixed and then go where there was work – anywhere.

Today had started out like most days. But after Mel stepped out from the soup kitchen door, something felt different. The sky had turned from light blue to a dark gray. The air was humid, and the first spits of rain were splattering on the sidewalk. The whole scene hinted of a torrential downpour. Cecily was probably back at the car.

As Mel ran, the rain began to pound down. With each crack of lightening, she ran faster, counting the seconds between the rumbling thunder and the light that followed. Her wet jeans tightened and stuck to her legs; the small patches of dry skin behind her knees began to sting. Her feet slipped in her flip-flops, causing her to trip and lose her grip on the large to-go container of soup. It sailed through the air and exploded on the sidewalk in front of her.

But for the moment, that didn't matter; getting back

to the Pinto and changing out of her wet clothes was the thing Mel wanted most. That's when she realized she'd forgotten to put the key back under the frame of the Pinto. She groaned when she thought of Cecily waiting in the rain and then ran faster.

8

Homeless

Mel wasn't sure at first if the pelting rain was blurring her view of the Pinto, or if the car had actually been moved. She slowed her pace to a jog, scanning the area where the Pinto had been parked. The clothes she'd carefully hung on the line that morning were lying limp and wet in the grass. Her favorite green sweater appeared to be immersed in a puddle.

Mel could see that Cecily wasn't there, but she called her name into the darkness of rain and thunder anyway. She ran back down the street, hoping to find her. For as far as Mel could see, the street going into town was empty. She turned and ran back to the overpass. Every few minutes, she called out Cecily's name, but no one answered.

As Mel's disappointment turned to anger, she stopped calling for Cecily and began to yell. "I! Hate! You! Cecily Tulley! You hear me? I hate you!" And she kept on yelling until the only thing left in her was sadness.

Exhausted, Mel collected the clothes she'd hung to

dry earlier in the day. She couldn't believe her blanket had been spared; it had been tucked next to the side of a pillar just enough to have remained mostly dry. Mel needed to get out of the rain. Sound moved in all directions under the overpass – even the sound of her flip-flops touching down on the asphalt echoed in the vacant space. She didn't remember it sounding this way when she'd explored The Pillars, as she called them, that first day. It had felt safe then. She tried to convince herself that this was the same place, and that the shivers running up and down her spine were caused by nothing more than the darkness and the rain.

Mel found a small cave-like place up behind one of the shorter pillars that supported the road above, and it gave her a vantage point to watch the street. It was hard to climb into the space with her wet jeans. She finally managed by running at the concrete wall, jumping, and pulling herself up with her fingertips until she could lift one leg onto the ledge and hoist herself up. She wrapped her blanket around her shoulders; but even so, she was unable to get warm – much less contain the salty tears pouring from her eyes. She thought about Fearless, and his window ledge, and she hoped that he'd either stayed in the soup kitchen or found a place to stay dry. The rain continued to pelt against the asphalt for what seemed like

an eternity, at times beating like a million drums in the
dark. Mel prayed for the rain to stop, and, to her surprise,
moments later it did. But what remained was silence, and
stillness, and although Mel tried to stay calm, her imagi-
nation filled the quiet with fear.

Why wasn't Cecily here? The question sat in front of
her, demanding an answer. Mel pushed it away. It pushed
back.

Mel curled up into a tighter ball, her arms wrapped
around her knees, her teeth chattering uncontrollably.
She was cold to the bone and too scared to move. *Cecily
would show up. She wouldn't just take off.*

Every now and again, Mel called Cecily's name and
listened as a hollow echo reverberated through the concrete pillars. It was an eerie sound, and the place felt
haunted, especially when the smell of menthol drifted
from somewhere. Mel hoped it was a sign. *Cecily would be
back soon.*

*She probably came, saw the car gone, and went looking
for me,* Mel thought. But that did little to console her
fear. What she knew for sure was that Cecily hadn't taken
the car – because Mel had the key. The only possibility
was that it was towed, or – a shiver shot straight up Mel's
spine – maybe Craig had found their campsite. Maybe
he'd come looking for his car; he was the only other

person who had a key. The more she thought about it, the more she feared Craig must have found the Pinto.

Mel quietly began to sing, hoping it would dissipate the fear, but she stopped when she realized that there might be others also taking shelter under the overpass. She began making lists in her head. As each list came to an end, she began another. She listed every book she could remember reading and every poem she'd memorized. She began spelling words, as many as she could that began with *a*, then *b*, then *c*, then *d*. She continued the list-making all night long, never stopping for fear she'd fall asleep and not hear Cecily's call when she came looking for her.

9

Waiting for Cecily

As the first bit of sun reached over the horizon, Mel stretched her aching arms and legs. *Enough waiting.* She was determined to find Cecily. She found a pen and an empty menthol cigarette package near the place the Pinto had been parked. She took the thin foil papers out that normally held the cigarettes in place, folded them, and tucked them into her pocket. The clear plastic sleeve on the pen was broken, but the little ink tube was intact. Mel carefully ripped apart the glued edges of the cigarette package until she had a flat piece of cardboard; the inside was mostly dry. She wrote Cecily a note. There had been a few other times that Mel had spent the night alone, when Cecily hadn't come home, but Cecily had always shown up the next day, and Mel was counting on that to be the case again.

Cecily,
I'll be right back. Please don't leave!

Love, Mel
PS. Where were YOU?

Mel gathered a collection of stones and grouped them in a circle. In the center, she placed the note; she added a small stone to hold it in place. She folded one of Cecily's shirts into the shape of an arrow, laid it on the ground so that it pointed at the circle, and headed toward town.

As Mel walked past the bakery, her stomach began to churn and it reminded her that it was Saturday and the soup kitchen was closed. She thought about all her money hidden under the floor mat. It was gone, too.

She continued walking up one street and down another all morning. At each alleyway, she called out Cecily's name, and on more than one occasion, she was sure she saw her. But each time, in the end, it was someone else.

On the corner of Olive and Fifth, the morning traffic was slow but steady. Mel went to her spot, stood tall, laid out her purple scarf in a circle, and she began to sing. The singing served two purposes. First, Mel could make a few dollars to get some breakfast. And second, there was also the chance Cecily was nearby and would hear her voice.

Mel didn't expect to see Rose. Her VW van came to an abrupt halt at the intersection, even though the traffic light shone green. Rose got out, oblivious to the cars that sped by and honked at her apparent disregard for traffic.

"I was starting to think you might be doing something crazy like this," Rose said as she lumbered toward her.

"It's not against the law to sing on the street," Mel said as she stared out at the cars pulling up to the intersection.

"You're a sitting duck for some creep," Rose shot back.

Rose was angry and it caught Mel off guard. There was a lot about this large, dark-skinned woman that no one would want to mess with.

Mel glanced nervously at Rose and then back to the street. She continued to sing, pushing the words of her song farther into the traffic. A woman walked by and threw three quarters and a couple of dimes onto the scarf.

"Thanks!" Mel said, taking a brief break from her song. Then she dared to look in Rose's direction.

"Standing out here isn't going to get you anything but trouble," Rose said. Her voice was softer now, deep.

Mel wanted to tell Rose right then and there that Cecily hadn't come home. But an almost instinctual warning sounded within her. *Don't do that.* It was Cecily's rule about not saying anything to anybody; Mel was to keep quiet and not share any information about herself or Cecily, about where they were living, what she had or didn't have for breakfast, or why she often arrived at school in clothes that were too small or miles too big. "Involve people, and before you know it, you'll be in foster care." That's what Cecily had said, and Mel knew from experience that sharing too much could cause a lot of trouble.

"Now, I'm inclined to mind my own business," Rose said, "but I'm starting to worry that you are on your own."

"My mom's at work," Mel answered, looking down at her feet. She knew Rose wasn't the kind of woman you could look at and lie to.

"Well, then I guess it would be okay for you to come on back to the kitchen," Rose said, "until your mom's finished working."

"But the kitchen is closed."

"I bake on Saturdays."

"Actually, I can't. I need to go back home. I'm meeting my mom for lunch."

"Can I give you a lift?" Rose asked.

"No. Thanks. It's not far," Mel said, glancing in the distance as if looking for her house in the myriad of buildings. "It's just over there a few blocks."

"Well, I'll be at the kitchen most of the day," Rose said. "Just knock on the back door and I'll let you in."

Mel nodded.

"I'll give you one of my fresh cinnamon buns," Rose said.

"Okay," Mel said. "I will."

"And I'll bet Fearless will be stopping by also," Rose added, giving yet another reason to come by.

Mel watched as Rose hiked back across the road, climbed into her van, and drove away. Everything about the way Rose spoke said one thing: she knew something was up.

Mel walked back to the overpass. Still no sign of Cecily. She crawled up into the small cave-like space where she'd spent the night before, and she stuffed a couple of dry shirts into a T-shirt, fashioning a pillow, and then wrapped herself up in the blanket. Her stomach wanted a cinnamon bun, but her body wanted sleep. It was easier to sleep in the day – especially in her little spot, her back tight against the wall, head resting on the makeshift pillow. She was warm.

10

The Strangers

It was almost dark when the strangers showed up. Their voices echoed through the pillars and woke Mel from her sleep.

"Well," one of the voices said, shining a light in Mel's general direction, "this must be the place, but I don't see a Pinto wagon and I don't see any sign of a kid."

"If she was here earlier, she's gone now," another voice said.

Then a familiar voice spoke. "Mel, it's Rose. Are you out there?"

Mel stole a peek at them from her spot. She could have tucked her head back in after she spotted Rose, but she didn't.

"My living, loving God, girl," Rose said as she caught sight of Mel and walked toward her. The other two followed.

Mel looked at the strangers. One was definitely a police officer. He reached out his hand; Mel kept hers tucked in her blanket.

"I'm Constable Hill and this is Ms. Jeffery," he said, gesturing to the woman who stood beside him. "She's a social worker, and I gather you know Rose."

Mel nodded.

"You'll need to come with us, Miss Tulley," said the officer.

"I can't. I'm waiting for my mom."

"Mel," Rose said, "your mom's in jail. She was picked up last night. She'd been drinking, and – I don't know – they're saying something happened with a store clerk. She may have been caught shoplifting."

As the words found their place in the cool night air, Mel accepted that she'd known this truth all along, but that she had tried to keep from thinking about it.

"These people are going to take you to your grandmother's."

Mel didn't respond. Instead, she pushed down all the sadness rising inside her.

Rose lifted her hands, palms up, and scanned the emptiness under the overpass. "You can't stay here, child," she said.

"This whole thing is Gladys's fault – she wouldn't open the door."

"Come on down," Rose said as she reached up toward Mel.

Mel shifted her body and hung her feet over the ledge. Getting down was much easier than getting up.

Rose tucked her hands under Mel's arms, lifting and then lowering her. Mel felt small, but she also felt safe, and it was such a welcome feeling – like that first gasp for air when you've been holding your breath for too long underwater. As Rose brought Mel to the ground, she continued to hold onto her, cocooning Mel in her thick arms.

"Here now," she whispered as she held Mel tight, "everything is going to be all right." Mel gave a deep sigh. And then she let each breath that followed carry away all the worry and fear and sadness that had been threatening to spill out of her for days, maybe even years. It wasn't the kind of cry you could stop and then start; it was a cry that came from a place so deep inside that for years, when Mel would look back at this moment, she would know that it changed something inside of her forever.

"Your mom called the mission, and they called Rose," the officer said. "And we've already spoken with your grandmother; she's expecting you."

Mel nodded, her head pressed against Rose's chest, and continued crying.

Constable Hill, Ms. Jeffery, and Rose helped Mel gather her things up and put them in the back of the police car. The backseat was quiet; the thick glass that separated the front from the back dulled the sounds of the engine and the conversation up front. Rose pulled Mel close, and Mel offered no resistance. Her sobbing eased and she found herself listening to the sounds of their collective breathing and the quiet hum of the tires on the road. It seemed like only minutes before the car pulled up to Gladys's.

Rose stayed in the car. Mel would have liked to stay with her.

"Everything is going to be okay," Rose whispered as Mel started to get out of the car. She set her hand on Mel's. "And I hope you'll come by the kitchen on occasion. I know Fearless will be waiting for a visit."

"I will," Mel answered as she stood up.

Ms. Jeffery handed Mel a backpack from the trunk of the car. "Here you go," she said.

Mel looked up at her, curious about the backpack and why it was being given to her.

"There's a toothbrush, some toothpaste, shampoo, a couple of granola bars, and a few other things you might need in there. It's yours to keep," Ms. Jeffery said.

As Constable Hill, Ms. Jeffery, and Mel entered the building, Mel looked up the staircase.

This time, there was no expectation. Mel knew she would call her "Gladys."

They climbed the twenty-four stairs and then walked the sixteen steps to Gladys's apartment. When Constable Hill knocked, Gladys opened the door. The apartment was dark and plain.

The front door led directly into the living room. A small off-centered archway led to the kitchen. On one side of the arch there was a polished wooden end table and a lamp, and next to that a brown couch with two circular pillows. The couch was pushed up against the window ledge, which caused the floor-length curtains to bunch up. Here and there were small stacks of dust-covered boxes that had been taped shut. The place looked as though Gladys had been planning to move, and then never did.

Across from the couch there was a bookshelf. What Mel noticed immediately was that there were no books on it – not a single one. Rather, there were rows of mismatched recycled boxes that were sealed shut with black tape. Mel could see dates scrawled onto the boxes in black or red felt marker. It was difficult to read any of them in the low light. There was no art on the wall – only what appeared to be either light green or gray wallpaper with a faint pattern. Mel glanced down at her armload of damp clothes and then remembered that her blanket was still under the overpass, but said nothing.

"Perhaps," Ms. Jeffery said, scanning the dark living room, "we could sit at the kitchen table."

Gladys walked into the kitchen, repositioned her chair so that it no longer faced the TV, and sat down. Constable Hill, Ms. Jeffery, and Mel followed. Gladys then got up, went back into the living room, and came back with a foldout chair.

"First time in nine years she bothers to come by," Gladys said as though defending her position.

Ms. Jeffery and Constable Hill nodded as Gladys spoke, but neither of them interrupted.

"Tux, my husband . . . her grandfather," Gladys said, tossing a glance in Mel's direction, "looked night and day. Cecily didn't have the decency to say where she was going; she just got up and left. And after all we'd done for her. And I can see, by what's gone on with Cecily in the past few days, that she hasn't learned a thing in the nine years she's been gone." This last statement Gladys spoke slowly, as though what she was saying was surely proving a point.

Mel wanted to defend Cecily. She wanted to say, "We were starting over; we were coming home – but you wouldn't open the door." But the words hid inside her.

She knew better than to say anything: it was obvious that Cecily was already in enough trouble.

Mel asked to use the bathroom, not because she needed to but because she wanted to get up from the table. Gladys motioned her head in the direction of the bathroom door. Mel stood and then set her clothes on her chair. It was uncomfortable being with the three adults all tiptoeing around whatever it was they needed to talk about.

When Mel opened the bathroom door, one thing was clear. Cecily was right: the bathroom was the nicest part of the apartment. The floors and walls were tiled with small white tiles. Just inside the door, a large, square, white porcelain sink sat on a rectangular pedestal. Beside it, a towel was neatly folded over a glass rod. Above the sink, clipped to the wall with silver clasps, hung a tall mirror, and Mel let her fingers run along the scalloped edges. Her eyes moved from the mirror to an ornate black radiator that was tucked into the corner, but it was nothing in comparison to the stand-alone cast iron bathtub that sat kitty-corner to it. The claw feet, which looked like bird talons grasping spheres, were definitely the most unique part of the tub. The bathtub's only flaw was a dripping faucet that left an orangey stain all the way from the tap to the drain. It had been more than a week, Mel realized, since she'd had a shower or bath.

As she turned toward the door, Mel noticed four thin lines on the lower half of the door frame; they appeared to be nothing more than little scratches in the white paint. She looked closer. They were actually words. *Melody 12 months*. She let her fingertips slide up the frame – *18 months*, then *24 months*, and then to a last mark, *36 months*. Her first, second, and third birthdays. She had stood here to be measured. Mel let her fingers run up the door frame, stopping at just above eye level. Without any thought, she turned, pressed her back to the frame, rested her palm on the top of her head, and then turned back to face her fingertips, which marked her height today – and the distance between then and now. She turned back, facing out from the frame to the room, to the tub, to the tiles. Nothing jarred her memory.

As she opened the door from the bathroom to the kitchen, all three adults looked in her direction. She couldn't help but feel guilty for having let herself explore the bathroom.

Ms. Jeffery and Constable Hill got up to leave. They each shook Gladys's hand and said good-bye to Mel. Ms. Jeffery mentioned that she would pick them up in the morning, to take them to court.

Gladys followed Ms. Jeffery and Constable Hill back into the living room. After they left, she locked the door.

Mel sat back down at the table, returning the small pile of clothes to her lap. *Maybe*, she thought, *Gladys would want to talk.*

Gladys walked back into the kitchen, shuffled past the table, and went into her room. Then she returned with a folded crocheted blanket. "You can use one of the pillows on the couch and this," she said as she handed Mel the blanket.

Gladys didn't say "Good night," or "Have a nice sleep," or that she was glad Mel was here. Rather, she lifted her chair and returned it to its place in front of the television. As Gladys reached to turn the television on, Mel stood up, walked to the living room, and placed her clothes on the floor. She then cautiously sat down on the couch, in some ways not completely certain that she could trust it to support her. After turning out the lamp, Mel covered herself up with the blanket, and let her head fall to the pillow. *Cecily hadn't just gone off. She'd sent Rose to find her. And if what Rose said was true, everything was going to be okay. She and Cecily would be together again soon.* Mel let her eyes close and she slept.

11

Your Honor

The large oak trees outside the courthouse windows cut the sun into a million little pieces. Each, Mel noticed, fell through the tall stained glass windows, landing like snowflakes on the tables, benches, and the polished plank floor. As her fingers followed the grain of the smooth wooden bench in front of her, Mel's eyes surveyed the other occupants of the courtroom. Other than Cecily, who was with her lawyer, Gladys, Constable Hill, Ms. Jeffery, and Rose, Mel didn't know any of the other ten to fifteen people in the courthouse. She mentally added the scene to her list of beautiful places. In fact, the room was so beautiful that, for a moment, Mel let herself forget why she was there. And without meaning to, she tuned out the judge's opening words.

"But, Your Honor," Cecily's lawyer said, "in fairness to the child, my client's daughter has never been before the court, and she may not be comfortable speaking to you directly."

"I suspect," the judge replied as he lifted his glasses off his nose and looked directly at the lawyer, "that twelve-year-old Melody Tulley is much older, and perhaps wiser, than her years, and is quite capable of speaking for herself."

Much older, perhaps wiser, Mel thought, letting those words dance around in her head. She took a deep breath and smiled – just a tiny smile – although a much larger smile sat beneath the surface, and then she rose and walked to the front of the court.

"Miss Tulley, I'm fairly certain that I have seen you on the corner of Olive and Fifth on a number of occasions. Is that so?"

From nowhere, Mel felt the heat growing within her. She nodded.

"Your Honor," Cecily's lawyer piped in again. "Can you be sure that it was Miss Tulley you saw on Olive and Fifth?"

The judge did not answer. Instead he turned to Mel. "Miss Tulley?"

Mel took in a quiet breath. Her emotions mixed around inside her. "Yes, Your Honor."

"And could you tell me what you were doing?"

"Singing, Your Honor."

"Yes, and . . ."

Mel could feel the hair on her head melting down into her scalp, warm and itchy and uncomfortable. She wanted to run, but couldn't have if she tried. She began to wonder if the shoplifting charge against Cecily was only part of the reason they were in court. Perhaps there had been some truth in the nightmare Mel had that first night in the Pinto. She hoped that Cecily would turn and look in her direction, offering a signal that everything was going to be okay.

The tingling patch of skin behind her knee began to sweat, and the sweat began to drip down the back of her calf. She wanted to – more than anything in that moment – reach down and wipe the salty snake off the back of her leg. But she didn't. And there was that tug on her head, not a real tug, but the kind of tug that makes you want to check your back, to check and be sure that the eyes you feel are on you are not actually on you. But Mel stood still, and now she was so uncomfortable she was unable to choke out a single word.

"Miss Tulley," the judge said, and then paused. "You are not in trouble. I only want to have a better picture of your life. It's important. You, Miss. You are important."

Mel noticed the judge's emphasis on *you*.

"I was singing for money," Mel began. "People walked by and they'd put money on my scarf. I always thanked them, Your Honor."

"That you did," the judge said. "You may be seated."

Mel wanted to say that Cecily *had* looked for a job, that she *had* looked everywhere. And that it was Mel's own idea to stand on the corner and sing this time, *not* Cecily's. But her mouth went dry, and an ever-expanding lump growing in her throat was keeping her from speaking. She thought back to times that she and Cecily were told by strangers "Pack it up! Move along!" They'd say "Get a job!" They'd ask, in a telling sort of way "Why aren't you in school?"

As Mel turned to walk back to her seat, she glanced at Cecily. Cecily closed and opened her eyes as she bit her lip. Mel knew the look; Cecily was sorry. Mel did a quick scan of the back of the courtroom. She spotted Rose again. Rose smiled and nodded. As Mel sat down beside Gladys, her thoughts went back to the words the judge left with her. "You, Miss. You are important." And the words landed on her here and there, just like the flaked sun falling through the paned glass.

The judge scanned the papers in front of him for a moment. Everyone sat, all waiting silently as the judge asked Cecily to stand. Then – even though she heard his words – Mel tried hard not to hear the judge's harsh comments for her mother. The judge spoke about Cecily being a poor role model to her daughter, the history of shoplift-ing. He spoke about the drug and alcohol abuse and about the risks of Mel and Cecily's lifestyle, and then he said that Cecily would be in jail for thirty days. Ms. Jeffery had mentioned in the car ride over to the courthouse that there was a chance that the sentence would be less than thirty days, or even – because of Mel – none at all. But she'd also prepared Mel for the worst, even if she hadn't said "worst-case scenario." But now, Cecily would be going to jail, and Mel would be staying on with Gladys.

"Ms. Tulley," the judge said, this time directly to Cecily, "are there any plans to enroll Melody in school in Riverview this September?"

Cecily didn't really answer the question. Instead she said, "Mel's been going to school."

For the most part, that was true. Mel had been in seventh grade for much of the year. It was only when they moved in with Craig, whose apartment was an hour's bus ride from school, that Cecily had decided it would be easier to just start at a new school in September – after all, there were only a couple of months left in the year.

"Yes, Ms. Tulley," the judge said to Cecily, "I don't doubt you have been schooling your daughter. But the education she receives "standing six" for you while you shoplift, or the education that your daughter is receiving on the corner of Olive and Fifth, is not the education she needs to get into college."

College. Mel moved the word around and around the inner workings of her mind. She'd never thought about college.

"So, Ms. Tulley, have you given any thought as to who will be able to care for your daughter in your absence?"

"Yes, Your Honor," Cecily said, tapping the table in front of her. "My mother, Gladys Tulley."

"Is she present in the court?"

"Yes, Your Honor."

"Gladys Tulley, will you come forward, please?" The judge's eyes passed quickly from Cecily to Gladys.

It was as though Mel was awakened from a deep sleep when her grandmother shuffled past her. Startled, Mel started to rise.

"Just sit *still*, child," Gladys grunted under her breath. Mel sat, and the heavy scent of mothballs, oozing from Gladys's suit, draped itself across her lap as Gladys pushed past Mel's knees.

Mel watched as Gladys pulled her shoulders back and raised her chin. She noticed how Gladys's thick, long tweed skirt was slightly twisted; the zipper at the waist and the open pleat at the hem were off to one side. This made the skirt, which was wide enough to accommodate someone with much broader hips, bulge and fold. Gladys passed through the same flakes of sun as she walked to the same place Mel had stood. They reflected light in Gladys's graying hair, then tumbled down her coat and skirt, and past the nylon stockings, which were pooling in rings just above Gladys's narrow ankles. The bits of light fell past her black shoes and onto the floor. Gladys then removed a white handkerchief from her coat pocket and wiped the sweat that dripped from her hairline and pasted her unruly gray hair to her forehead. Mel was lost in watching.

"Miss," the woman next to Mel whispered. "They're talking to you."

Mel immediately stood. "Yes, Your Honor?"

"Miss Tulley, do you understand that your grand-mother will be taking care of you for the duration of your mother's incarceration, and if need be for the duration of her probation? Your grandmother will provide you with a safe place to live, sufficient food, and proper supervision. At the end of that time, if your mother is able to secure proper housing, I expect you'll be able to live with her."

Mel nodded. It was going to be the worst-case scenario.

"Miss Tulley, are you willing to live with your grandmother?"

"Yes, Your Honor."

"One final question," the judge said as he looked directly at Mel. "Is there anything you need?"

Need. For as long as Mel could remember, there had always been things she needed. But it didn't seem to her that these were the things the judge was asking about. Perhaps it was the words *important* and *college*, dancing around in her head, that led Mel to think of the place most important to her – the library. What came to mind were the other people she would see there – kids her age and younger, all thumbing through their choices of books from tens of thousands if not a million different titles. Their parents suggesting books, and the young girls brushing aside their mothers' suggestions. Then watching them all do what had become impossible for her. They would take their selections up to the circulation desk, sign them out, and take them home. After the other kids were gone, Mel would walk up and down the aisles of books, softly suggesting the ones they left behind. "How about this one?" Or she would whisper, "This looks like a good book." She thought about the teenage boy she saw regularly at the library – Sleeping Beauty. Like her, he didn't ever seem to check out any books.

"Miss," the judge repeated. "Is there anything you need?"

Mel looked directly at the judge's bench. "A library card, Your Honor." It was a ticket into a world she had longed for, a ticket back to the best times she could remember.

"A library card?" The judge smiled as he repeated the words.

Gladys said, "Oh, for crying out . . ." And she heard the collective chuckle of the other people in the court-room. Once again, the dry patch of skin on her calf began to sting, but not so much. Mostly, she felt the excited pounding of her heart in her chest.

"Yes, Your Honor," Mel said, "a library card."

"I believe I just might be able to help you with that. Should I assume that you know the location of the down-town library?"

"Yes, Your Honor." Mel's back began to tingle.

The judge then listened to Cecily's lawyer as he addressed the bench. "But who'll be responsible for the books when they go missing, Your Honor? I certainly hope it will not be my client, who will be in incarcerated, or my client's mother, who lives on a very modest income."

"I'm sure I can count on Miss Tulley to return the books on time. Yes, Miss Tulley?" The judge looked back to Mel and gave a slight smile.

"Yes, Your Honor."

"Then we will adjourn."

Cecily's lawyer stood, then Cecily, and the two of them started to walk quickly from the courtroom. Mel watched as they came closer; she waited for Cecily to look at her, but Gladys stood up just as Cecily passed by, blocking Mel's view. Mel began to fear that they would take Cecily away before she had a chance to say good-bye. She tried to squeeze past Gladys. Gladys immediately wrapped her gnarled fingers tightly around Mel's slender arm and held her there until most of the people in the courthouse had left. Then Gladys briskly led Mel toward the exit, and it seemed as though they were going to march directly past Cecily, who was standing just outside the door, smoking.

"I'd say I've just about heard it all . . . a library card . . . my lord . . ." Gladys didn't quite finish her sentence, interrupted perhaps by the furrowed brow of the lawyer facing them.

Mel stopped and resisted Gladys's pull to keep moving when they reached the door. She lifted her free hand, reached across her body, and was about to remove Gladys's grip from her arm. But before she could, Gladys let go of her.

"I'm so sorry, Mel. I never meant for this to happen," Cecily said as she leaned into Mel, blowing the exhaled cigarette smoke over Mel's head and shoulders. It was their little ritual, Cecily's way of surrounding her with a white light of protection. Mel didn't like the smell of smoke, but it did, in its own weird way, make her feel safe.

"I'll write to you," Cecily whispered.

Mel nodded.

"And we'll find a place just as soon as I'm back," Cecily added. She said it as though she was going on a trip somewhere. "I promise."

Mel bit hard on her top lip; Cecily often made promises. Silent tears flowed full force from Mel's eyes, spilling down her cheeks into the small crevasses of her mouth. Cecily's lawyer reached into his coat and gave Mel a piece of tissue, and then he fumbled around in his pocket, patting it as though he was looking for something.

Ms. Jeffery came by. "It might not be the full thirty days," she told Gladys. "Good behavior and all . . ."

"The bus will be here any minute," Gladys said as though she hadn't heard Ms. Jeffery's comment.

Cecily's lawyer took a step toward Gladys and whispered that it would be good to give Cecily a few more minutes with Mel.

Cecily wrapped her arm around Mel's shoulders, squeezing her tighter than Mel could ever remember being hugged. As she kissed the top of Mel's head, Mel leaned into her. Cecily finally released the squeeze, letting her hand gently slide down off Mel's shoulder, down her arm, past her elbow and wrist, and finally to Mel's fingertips. Cecily glanced in the direction of the lawyer as though she was making sure that he wasn't watching, and she discretely slid two bills, rolled like little cigarillos, into Mel's hand. Mel knew what was happening; she could feel the smooth bills as they unfurled into her fingertips. Cecily glanced back in the direction of her lawyer.

"Quick!" Cecily whispered.

Mel tucked her hand into her pocket, knowing that wherever the money had come from, it wasn't rightfully Cecily's – nor was it rightfully hers.

"It's time for them to go," Cecily's lawyer said, turning from Gladys toward Cecily.

"White light," Cecily said as once again she blew smoke over Mel's head and shoulders.

"You too," Mel answered as she turned to follow Gladys.

The first time she looked back, Cecily was in the same place, watching her leave. The second time, Cecily's head was down and her lawyer was still going through his jacket pocket. The third time, Cecily was gone.

Mel's thoughts went back to last December and the day at Sunset Food Market. Cecily was caught stealing a bag of mini Swiss cheese rounds, three cans of smoked oysters, and a half-dozen mandarin oranges. When the young store clerk left the office to get the manager, Mel couldn't believe what she was seeing when Cecily snapped up one of the cans of oysters from the desk and quickly slipped it into Mel's pocket.

When the store manager had come into the office, he had said without even looking at Cecily that *they* were all the same, all looking for a free ride. If Mel's pocket hadn't been home to a can of stolen oysters, she might have defended herself. But instead, it took all she had not to set it back on the table and run.

She thought about all this as she and Gladys walked to the bus stop. She wished that Ms. Jeffery was driving them home. Once at the bus stop, Mel sat down on one end of the bench. Gladys, on the other hand, was grumbling. She removed her hat and undid her coat – all the while complaining about the sun being too bright, the day being too hot, and her shoes being too tight.

It was all going by Mel until Gladys blurted out in exasperation, "For crying out loud, a library card!"

Yes, Mel thought, *a library card*. She began making a mental list of all the books she'd seen over the last week that she wanted to check out.

—

"Wake up!" Gladys said. "The bus is here."

Mel wanted to say that she wasn't asleep, that she was thinking, but she didn't. Gladys, once again, took hold of her arm. The whole exercise was a combination of being leaned on and hoisted up into the bus.

"She rides for free," Gladys said, jerking her head toward the fare schedule.

The sign clearly read "Children nine and under free." Gladys then poured the contents of a rumpled envelope into the coin slot and continued down the narrow aisle. The driver gave her a doubting nod, and Mel felt her face flush.

"Here," Gladys said, pointing to the seat next to the back exit. "Sit down." Everything about the way Gladys spoke told Mel that Gladys was angry.

Mel was grateful to have the window seat. The view would keep her from thinking about the grumbling in her empty stomach. If today was the first day, then there were twenty-nine more days, but if the judge counted the two days Cecily had already been in jail, then today was twenty-seven, tomorrow would be twenty-six, and maybe with good behavior . . .

Mel knew that staying at Gladys's wasn't going to be anything to look forward to. Nothing Gladys said or did made Mel think that she was welcome or that this could be her home – even if it was just for a month. Gladys was cold, and Mel wondered about Gladys's anger toward Cecily, about how it was connected to Tux dying and the jewelry box and everything else that had happened, and if there were any answers stored in all the little boxes that lined the walls and encircled the room of the apartment. And if now, with Mel there, Gladys had reason to set that anger loose.

Mel's family wasn't like the families she read about in books, the stories that had fueled the thoughts she'd carried up the stairs that first day she and Cecily arrived back in Riverview. That day, there had been hopes of baked cookies, warm hugs, and kind words. But those dreams had tumbled down the stairs, and Mel had no intention of picking them up again – ever.

Gladys showed no sign of making dinner when they arrived back at the tiny apartment. Rather, she sat down in the kitchen, and turned on the TV. Mel sat on the sagging couch and looked at the deadbolts on the door, the tinfoil on all the windows, the stacks of dusty, yellowing newspapers tightly tied with string that were piled next to a box of flattened Red Label milk cans and neatly folded orange pekoe tea boxes.

She slipped her hand into her pocket, brought out the two twenty-dollar bills, and then promptly put them back. When she walked into the kitchen, Gladys seemed oblivious to her presence. With the tinfoil on the windows, blocking the afternoon sun that might have shone in Gladys's apartment, and with only the small fluorescent light flickering on the stove, the tiny apartment was in perpetual dusk.

Mel looked at the white metal enamel cupboard that was strangely positioned in front of a door that led off the kitchen, as though the room didn't exist. *What is with that room?* she thought.

With a deep breath, Mel garnered the courage to be heard over the TV, and, almost shouting, she asked, "Is it okay if I go for a walk?"

"Where?" Gladys barked back.

"Just down the street."

"There isn't anything but trouble for you to get into on this street," Gladys said.

"I was just —"

"You can pick me up two cans of milk at Frohberger's. But I tell you, girl, if you try pulling one of your mother's stunts, I'll let them toss you in that cell with her and throw away the keys."

Ignoring this, Mel asked, "Is it Red Label milk that you want?"

"Yes, and I know exactly how much it is, so don't try pulling any fast ones on me." Gladys set three dollars on the table and turned back to the TV.

Going to Frohberger's would give Mel the opportunity to change one of the twenties into coins and bills so that she had bus money. It would also satisfy her growing curiosity about Mr. Frohberger, her grandfather, and the store.

12

Frohberger's

The Frohberger's sign hung out from the long, narrow building on the corner of Maple and Thirty-Seventh. A bright red wrought-iron bike rack sat empty under an enormous oak tree shading curved concrete steps. Inside, the long, wide planks of wood floor were smooth and inviting. There was a barrel of damp sawdust next to the door. An old man was sprinkling scoops full of the sawdust onto the floor and then sweeping it up. Single lightbulbs in metal shades hung from the high ceiling, illuminating the extra-wide aisle that separated one row of shelves from the other. As Mel took in the sights of the store, the old man finished sweeping and then shuffled to a place behind the counter next to an elaborate cash register. The store was what Mel imagined a store would have looked like a hundred years ago. The smell was sweet, and, as Mel breathed in the cool air, the corners of her mouth lifted, and she smiled. She wondered if the old guy was Mr. Frohberger.

The floorboards gave long creaks as Mel made her way past the sparsely stocked shelves. There were two or three of most things. She'd already passed the cans of Red Label, but she kept walking. She made a mental list of the products she liked: cereal (four kinds), macaroni and cheese, chocolate chip cookies, gingersnaps, ketchup, mustard, relish, canned ravioli, chicken noodle soup, pork and beans, salsa, corn chips, barbecue chips, instant rice.

At the end of the aisle there was a small cooler with four jugs of milk, three packages of cheese slices, and two cartons of eggs. Next to it was a freezer. It was difficult to see exactly what was hidden under all the white ice that grew around the edges.

At the back of the store hung floor-length black velvet curtains. They were the kind of curtains used in theaters. Mel wanted to peek behind them, but she didn't. What Cecily had told her about Tux's Saturday Magic Matinees must have been true. She let her fingers run down a fold of velvet, but not for long. Mel felt the shop-keeper's eyes on her back, and it was an uncomfortable feeling she was all too familiar with.

She made an about-turn, picked up the cans of Red Label on her way to the front, and set them next to the newspapers on the counter. Mel noticed the collection of four-leaf clovers pressed under the thick glass. There were seven of them – Cecily's lucky number. There wasn't much behind the counter: chocolate bars, small packets of pain relievers, lottery tickets, gum, ballpoint pens, a few plastic tubs of penny candies, and assorted bags of chips. An old cardboard display, hanging slightly lopsided on the wall, held a few last pairs of cheap sunglasses.

"Will that be everything?" the storekeeper asked.

"I was wondering if I could also get some change?"

"Oh, sure. What do you need – dimes or nickels?" the storekeeper asked as he pushed a large key on the ornate cash register.

The register clunked, a gear was released somewhere within the enormous contraption, and it produced a clear and precise *ka ching!* as the cash drawer opened. Mel had never seen or heard anything like it.

"Well, actually, this –" Mel put the three dollars on the counter, "is for the canned milk. I need to bring that change back to my grandmother. I was . . ."

"Your grandmother?" the storekeeper interrupted. "Who would that be?"

"Gladys Tulley."

"Gladys. So you're her granddaughter?"

"Yes," Mel said, and in that moment she decided to find another place to get change for the bus.

As the storekeeper counted the change back, he set

each coin on the counter. "Two-fifty, seventy-five, and three."

An unusual look moved across the storekeeper's face. He looked down, and then his head turned slightly to the side. "You're Melody?"

"Yes, I am."

"Cecily's daughter?"

"Yes."

"Well, how about that. It's been a long time. I don't suppose you remember me. My name's Ed Frohberger. I knew you when you were knee-high to a grasshopper."

Mel laughed at the thought of being that small.

"I was a good friend of your grandfather. Thirty years Tux and I were friends." As he spoke, Mr. Frohberger pulled a half-filled plastic container off the shelf and used the little tongs to fish out a multi-colored gummy. "Here you go, Miss Melody. Welcome back to the neighborhood."

"Thank you," Mel said, but what she really wanted to do was ask him to tell her more.

"My pleasure," Mr. Frohberger answered. "It'll be great for Gladys to have someone around to run errands for her. Give her my regards."

"I will," Mel garbled out as she tried to chew the almost-rock-hard candy.

Once outside, Mel looked up at the stately trees and worn-down houses. She couldn't help but wonder what it might be like to be one of these trees, or even to be Mr. Frohberger, or even Gladys. *What does it feel like to be in the same place today as you were yesterday, as you will be tomorrow?* Cecily liked change. Lots of it. Mel, on the other hand, did not.

As Mel sauntered down the street to the market, she kicked little bits of chipped concrete from the lifting and tilting sidewalk. When she got there, she picked out a bag of chips, and – although it didn't feel right using what she was sure was the lawyer's money – she did it anyway and got the change she needed: three five-dollar bills and the rest in quarters. She'd break the five-dollar bills one at a time as she needed them.

"My neighborhood," Mel whispered. "This was my neighborhood."

She liked the sound of those words strung together, and she felt happy all the way back to Gladys's – until she tried the door to the apartment. It was locked.

"You can't be leaving the door unlocked when you go!" Gladys snarled as she opened the door. "I'm giving you a key, and I expect you to hang on to it. It's for the top lock. If you lose it, you'll have to pay to have the lock changed." Gladys took the too-short string she'd threaded through the hole at the top of the key and stretched it over Mel's head. Then, using one hand to take the cans of Red Label evaporated milk from Mel, she held out her other palm. "Change," she said.

Mel lifted the key up, dropped it between her shirt and her skin, and then handed Gladys the coins.

"You can put your stuff on that bottom shelf, but don't be getting into any of those boxes." Gladys motioned to the vacant end of the bookshelf that sat across from the couch. "I'll be leaving for work at six-thirty first thing tomorrow morning," Gladys added, and then strode into the kitchen.

Scenes, like those in a film, sometimes played out in Mel's mind. In this scene, Gladys was telling Mel once again not to touch any of her things. Words ran along the bottom of the screen, like captions.

There is a way they treat you when they don't trust you, or don't want to trust you. It's in the way they speak, the words they use, the way they hold their body and look at you. Sometimes they look at you for so long it feels like forever, like they have already caught you doing what they think you are going to do, or have already done. Other times, they look past you or through you as though you are invisible.

Mel's eyes returned to Gladys, who was futzing in the kitchen, and then to her backpack, and then to the shelf.

13

Tinfoil Sky

Late that night, with the crocheted blanket wrapped tightly around her, Mel peeled back a corner of the tinfoil from the window beside the couch, and looked out at the stars. Air – cool, clean, and fresh – blew through a thin crack in the paned glass window. If there was a window where Cecily was, Mel was sure Cecily would be looking up at the night sky and thinking about her, too. Mel brought a handful of her spiraled ringlets close to her face. Her hair still smelled of the menthol cigarette smoke Cecily blew over her head at the courthouse.

She thought about the list Cecily would be making. It would be a list of all the things they would do when this was over – when things got better. Cecily was going to come by and get her, and together they were going to find a place of their own. They'd make a list of places they'd like to live, a list of all the details of the perfect home, and a list of things they'd need.

"You have my heart, girl," Cecily would tell her.

"You're my grounding force. You're my gift from God Almighty Himself." Then Cecily would start singing: "I need you, like the flower needs the rain, you know I need you" – or some other silly love song. Cecily's voice always made Mel smile when she was sad. It made her feel warm when she was cold, and it made her feel safe when she was scared. And when Cecily was finished singing, she'd say, "Girl, let's write a list." The list would include all the places they were going to tour when they got enough money together to cut their first record, a list of festivals they'd sing at, and a list of songs they were going to sing – in the order they were going to sing them. Mel always went along with it, but what she didn't tell Cecily was that – secretly – she hoped they'd find one beautiful place, and they'd stay there. They'd have a garden, flowers, and, maybe, if Cecily could afford it, Mel could get a kitten.

Cecily talked about being onstage, in front of thousands of people, and about jamming with other musicians backstage as though it was destined to happen. It would be Cecily's moment of fame. When Cecily talked about her dream, Mel always felt guilty, wondering if she had been the reason Cecily hadn't been able to pursue her dream. Cecily had only once told her about the moment everything changed. Cecily had been drinking and let the words slip out. She said that everything had been going great, that she was on her way, playing lots of festivals, that there had been talk of a record. But then Cecily had started partying a lot, and the next thing she knew, she was pregnant.

But Mel didn't want to think about that, and she let her mind wander back to Frohberger's. If Cecily had been there today, she'd have seen the four-leaf clovers. They would have been a sign of impending good luck. Mel wanted to believe it was true.

Pulled back into the present, Mel heard someone or something stumbling up the stairs and then down the hallway just outside the apartment door. She quickly unfolded the little piece of tinfoil and pressed it back against the cool windowpane, eliminating the sliver of light it afforded. She tucked her head under the crocheted blanket, breathing in her own steamy breath, and she waited. Her fingers traced the pleats of the threadbare satin pillow, and her other hand clutched the key to the door. The little apartment wasn't big, it wasn't fancy, but there were doors, and they were locked, and she was safe.

When all the noise moved behind a closed door down the hall, Mel got up from the couch and checked the deadbolts. All but one was set; duct tape prevented it from locking. Surprised that all the yelling hadn't woken Gladys up, she tiptoed back to the couch, rearranged the pillows, lay down, and tucked the satin pillow under her head. It was early morning before she heard another sound.

Mel woke to Gladys pushing on her shoulder.

"Get up! You're going to make me late for work."

As Mel sat up and looked at Gladys, she noticed the words "Fan's Dry-Cleaning" embroidered on the front of Gladys's smock. Gladys was still working at the cleaners.

Mel pulled on her jeans, leaving on the T-shirt that doubled as pajamas. She slipped her feet into her flip-flops, lifted her backpack over her shoulder, took the plate and toast from Gladys's outstretched hand, and walked through the doorway and into the hall. Mel thought that she must be going to work with Gladys.

"Slide the plate under the door when you're finished," Gladys said after she locked not only the top lock, the one Mel had a key for, but also the bottom lock, using a different key.

"You're locking me out?" Mel asked.

"No, I'm locking my things in," Gladys snapped back.

"I have no intention of taking any of your things," Mel said.

Gladys drew in a stiff breath, as though she was somehow justified in leaving her granddaughter out in the hallway.

Only after she had taken seven steps – Mel counted them – and was about to turn the corner and walk down the main hall, did Gladys pause. She turned, walked back, and unlocked the bottom lock, the lock that Mel didn't have a key for. "I guess it doesn't really matter," she hissed. "Your mother took most of what had any value."

Mel didn't look at her. She gave no indication that she'd heard what Gladys had said, or that she was grateful to have access to Gladys's apartment. Instead, she stared out the window. What she thought of adding to Gladys's proclamation was *Cecily isn't only my mother; Cecily is also your daughter.*

She listened to the sounds of Gladys's shoes snapping on the stairs. As the downstairs door opened, a breeze swept through the hall, carrying with it dust from the floor and stairs. Mel felt it whisk by her on its way to the partially open hall window beside her. From her vantage point, she watched Gladys walk down the sidewalk, cross the street, and sweep past Frohberger's. Mel didn't expect her to look back, or maybe she did. Either way, she felt a guilty streak run up her back when Gladys, upon turning the corner toward the bus stop, cast a quick glance directly at the window.

Mel slid to the floor, her back against the wall, and ate her toast. When she was done, she removed the key that hung around her neck and set it on the plate with the crumbs from the toast.

"You can keep your key, Gladys Tulley," Mel whispered as she slid the key and plate under the door of the apartment.

Mel surveyed the hallway. The library wouldn't open for three hours. She closed her eyes and thought about which books she would check out, and before long drifted into a light sleep.

Two sets of footsteps could be heard racing through the hall and then down the stairs.

"Come on! We're going to miss the bus!" someone called out.

Mel realized it might be the same bus she needed to get to the library. She stood up, grabbed her bag, raced out of the building, and followed the two young men to the bus stop. The two men got on the first bus, but Mel sat on the bench and waited. According to the posted schedule, the Downtown 42 would be along in ten minutes. She was the only person to get on the bus when it arrived.

The winding bus route followed along the river, and Mel watched the usual mix of nicely dressed people, their coffees in hand, move promptly toward their shops and offices. The bus made stops at the courthouse and the community center. Mel saw a few people asleep on benches; others pushed loaded shopping carts filled with their belongings. The driver pulled up to the stop by the soup kitchen and waved to a few regulars as they dismounted. The library was just ahead. The excitement of checking out the books she'd been yearning for was becoming difficult to contain.

Mel didn't think about not getting a library card. She didn't think about anything stopping her from having one. But she quickly realized that she had never thought about how she would actually get the card. At least until her eyes met those of the librarian. "Hi, I'm Mel . . ." she said, her voice quivering with anticipation.

"Ah, so *you're* Miss Tulley," the librarian said. "Well, how about that. I've seen you in here recently, right?"

Mel was caught off guard. She hadn't realized that anyone had noticed her daily visits. She read the name on the tag of the woman's vest: Marilyn.

"Great! Let's get started," Marilyn continued. "Most of the paperwork is already filled out. I need one thing, though: an address and phone number for your grandmother. Did you bring that with you?"

"No . . . I didn't." Mel lifted one foot and ran the tip of her flip-flop down the back of her other leg to the floor.

She curled her toes into the soles of her feet and drew in a deep breath. The embarrassment was drowning her; she was going to have to divulge that a judge had granted her the card. "Your Honor, the judge . . . ," Mel started to explain.

"Oh yes, I know. Judge Pullman is a friend of mine. He's already had someone come in to sign for your card. I just need a phone number and an address to fill in the forms properly. Can you remember any part of it?"

The librarian's voice was kind, but in that moment, Mel couldn't even remember the street name, let alone the number.

"Okay, so how about you go ahead and pick out the books you want, and I'll put them on hold for you."

"No, thanks. I'll come back."

"Are you sure? It's not a problem for me to do this."

"I'm sure."

Mel left the library empty-handed and began the long walk back to Gladys's apartment. The return trip took an hour, partially because she walked so slowly. Mel did the math: thirty-nine dollars would give her at least thirty trips from Gladys's to the library. If Cecily was in jail for thirty days, and if it took them a month to find a place to live, the money wouldn't last. If Mel walked one way every trip, and didn't go every day, thirty-nine dollars could last two months. And maybe there'd be a bit left over to spend on things they'd need for their apartment. And there was no use rushing; Gladys wasn't home, the door was locked, and Mel no longer had a key.

Mr. Frohberger was standing behind the counter when Mel walked by the store. He waved and smiled. She couldn't help but wave and smile back.

Mel continued to Gladys's. She made a mental note of the building number, relieved to have at least one piece of information for the librarian. She climbed the stairs, walked down the hallway, turned the corner, and sat down across from the apartment door. The apartment number, an old-fashioned 2, had been removed, but a clear outline of it remained just below the brass peephole on the varnished wooden door.

Mel leaned her head back against the wall; her stomach reminded her that she was hungry. "I should have gone by the soup kitchen first," she whispered into the vacant hallway. But with the sun shining through the window and onto her face, she drifted into a place halfway between wakefulness and sleep.

"What?" Gladys asked when she saw Mel sitting outside the apartment door. "Didn't like any of those books at the library?"

Mel started at the sound of Gladys's voice, then turned her face up to the window, eliminating the possibility that Gladys could look down on her.

She doubted Gladys ever went to the library, but still, Gladys's voice cut the little excitement that remained of the day into pieces, and Mel could feel them disappearing into the dark and dusty corners of the hall. She decided not to ask Gladys for her phone number. Instead, Mel planned to find all the information she needed in the apartment, and look at it without Gladys knowing. The librarian hadn't asked for a signature; the judge had seen to that. All Mel needed was an address and phone number. It was a formality.

Gladys unlocked the door and pushed it open. The small plastic plate and key appeared. Gladys bent down and picked up the plate, then walked inside and into the kitchen. She said nothing about the key.

Moments later, she reentered the living room. "So what? Now you don't want the key?"

"No," Mel told her. "I don't. I'd rather wait in the hall."

"Well, fine then." Gladys paused, and Mel knew Gladys was readying herself to launch another attack. "But if I were you, I wouldn't be burning any bridges because the only thing you got going for you right now . . . is me."

Mel turned to stare at the drapes that hung in front of the window, as though she could see through them, past the tinfoil to the sky.

What stung the most was that it was true. There were no aunts, no uncles, no cousins. There was only Cecily and Gladys, and Cecily was in jail.

"And didn't I tell you to take the papers and cans down to Frohberger's the other day when you picked up the milk?"

Mel didn't answer. Instead, she picked up the top stack of newspapers and set a box of flattened cans on top.

"Is there anything you need?" Mr. Frohberger asked when she dropped off the last box of flattened cans – it had taken three trips to get them all. Only a few days ago, the judge had asked her the same question.

"No, thank you," Mel answered. "I'm just dropping these off."

She left the store and walked slowly back to the apartment. The door was locked. Mel knocked, then waited. Eventually, Gladys obliged. This would become a contest for control between them – Mel refusing the key and Gladys refusing to rush. Eventually, Gladys chose to leave the door unlocked each afternoon until Mel's return, so as not to be interrupted.

Mel went into the kitchen and reached for the broom behind the door. If she was going to be spending her mornings in the hall, it would be nice to at least sweep up the thick layer of dust.

"Where you going with that?" Gladys's voice was full of accusation.

"I thought I'd sweep the stairs and the hallway in front of your door."

"No, you're not taking my good broom out there. If you want to sweep the hall, use the broom at the bottom of the stairs."

Mel found the worn-out straw broom tucked in an alcove beside the front door at the bottom of the stairs. As she swept, she imagined the home she and Cecily would find. Today's vision was a little house, set on a piece of grass at the end of a lane, with a garden. Other times, home was an apartment, on the fortieth floor of a high-rise apartment building. Sometimes, especially when they were out in the cold, it was simply a warm place, any place safe.

Today, it seemed okay to dream. Cecily had promised, and – Mel didn't know why – this time she believed her. They were going to have a home of their own, even the judge had said so. And if being here for a month meant they'd have a place of their own when Cecily came back, Mel could stand it.

14

Caught

The phone hung by the kitchen cupboard next to the bathroom door. But the phone number, which was written in pen behind the little plastic rectangle on the base of phone, was impossible to read. She'd have to wipe it with a cloth to see the number. Mel decided to wait until long after Gladys went to bed to look at the phone again. Her plan was to sneak into the kitchen, wipe the phone panel in the dark, turn on the light really fast, and memorize the number before turning off the light again. She could be back on the couch within seconds.

Mel was sure the fan, humming away behind the door to Gladys's bedroom, would cover any noise she made fumbling around in the dark. With the tinfoil blocking any light from the moon, or streetlights, or passing cars, the place would be pitch-black.

Mel didn't remember the step stool that sat just inside the kitchen doorway, and, before she knew it, she was on the floor. Her head hit the countertop on the way down. Within seconds, Gladys was up.

"What the . . ." Gladys's door flew open, her flashlight swinging.

Mel's eyes strained to find Gladys behind the glaring light.

"Whatcha doing snooping around in here?"

Mel could feel Gladys's words striking her chest.

"You listen. You get off that floor and get outta here. Git!"

Mel got herself up onto her hands and knees, crawled to the living room, and climbed up onto the couch. She wasn't sure if Gladys meant for her to get out of the apartment or just out of the kitchen.

She tried hard not to hear Gladys yelling, telling her that she was going to call the judge first thing in the morning. Instead, Mel gently lowered her head into the folds of the satin pillow, being careful not to put any pressure on the bump forming on her forehead. She closed her eyes and let her fingers slip toward the center of the cushion where all the tucks of satin met under the smooth button. *The judge had to have counted the first two days. Twenty-five days to go.*

Mel made a mental list of all the songs she and Cecily loved to sing, and then she sang them silently to herself until she fell asleep.

—

"Get up!" Gladys yelled from the doorway to the kitchen. "Get yourself off that couch and in here right now!"

Mel knew what she needed to do next. She needed to lie. She was going to look Gladys straight in the face and lie.

"I'm sorry about last night, Gladys. I know I shouldn't have gotten up. I wanted to sneak something from the fridge."

This, Mel knew, was critical. She couldn't just say she was making her way to the bathroom, couldn't just say she was getting a drink of water. She needed to confess to something that she knew Gladys would be angry about, but it couldn't be about Gladys's things and it couldn't involve the library card.

Gladys didn't reply. Mel was relieved for the silence. *Twenty-four days.*

When Mel came out of the bathroom, Gladys was finishing her tea. The key sat on the table next to the plate with the toast, as though waiting for Mel. Mel picked up the plate and ignored the key. Gladys walked to the door. Mel followed her out, then sat down in the corner of the hall, under the window. Gladys didn't seem to notice the bruise on Mel's forehead; Mel told herself that it didn't matter. But what she also knew, though she didn't

want to think it, even to herself, was that it did matter:
grandparents were supposed to care.

"You don't need to call the judge," Mel said quietly.
"I won't do it again."

Gladys didn't answer; the sounds of Gladys locking
the door were deafening. Mel's eyes fell to the floor and
she let her fingertips follow the grain in the wood.

*The growth rings in trees tell you how old the tree is;
that's what makes the grain in wood. No two trees are exactly
the same. The rings are like fingerprints.*

Mel looked up again when Gladys had turned the
corner. The shadow of the leaves coming through the
window fell dark on the wall. The sun was shining. She
finished her toast, slid the plate under the door, and left
the building. Mr. Frohberger would know Gladys's phone
number.

"Well, let's see," Mr. Frohberger said as he glanced down
at a list by his telephone. "This is it right here." Pulling
a pencil from behind his ear, he jotted the number down
on a slip of paper. Mel thanked him – grateful he hadn't
asked her why she couldn't get the information from
Gladys – and left for the bus stop.

Once at the library, Mel took the steps two at a time
and swung the front door open. She saw the librarian as

she approached the circulation desk. "I've got it!" she blurted out in Marilyn's direction. "Apartment 2, 410 West Maple . . ."

"Great!" Marilyn answered. "Let's get this done."

Mel watched as Marilyn filled in the forms.

"Here you go," she said. "Sign the back, and I'll laminate it for you."

In her best handwriting, Mel deliberately wrote her full name, Melody Anastasia Tulley.

"Anastasia. That's a beautiful name. Is it a family name?" Marilyn asked.

"Maybe," Mel answered. "I'm not sure."

"Well, either way, it's beautiful."

When Marilyn returned with the card, Mel held it to her cheek. It was warm and smooth and it made her think about Cecily, about how, when Mel was little, Cecily would always say "It's great to be home!" whenever they walked into the library.

Mel hummed as she walked down the long, narrow aisles of books, her fingers tapping the spines like piano keys. The song "It's Beginning to Look a Lot Like Christmas" was terribly unseasonable, she noted, but she hummed on anyway. Everything was wonderful; she was in the library. She was there as a patron, a card-carrying patron, and she intended to take full advantage of her privileges. Mel wondered briefly about Sleeping Beauty, if she would see him, if he would notice her.

She took her time with each book she pulled from the shelf. Her fingers traced the edges. Some, she noticed, hadn't been opened in years, and others were well worn, their edges tattered and pages yellowed. There was no reason to rush. Altogether she could borrow fourteen books, but it was more than she wanted to carry to Gladys's. Cecily would have loved songbooks and travel books; Mel picked out two for her, not because she could get them to Cecily or anything. She did it just because she could. She found *The Last Battle*, the book she'd been saving to read but was forced to leave behind when she and Cecily had fled Craig's place.

Once Marilyn helped her check out her books, Mel turned and walked to the front exit. She was almost afraid to push the large arched door open, but she did. She counted as she walked down the stairs: one, two, and three. She continued to count each step as she proceeded down the cobbled sidewalk. Four, five, six. Still, no one stopped her. Seven. She walked toward the concrete picnic table. Eight, nine. She sat down. Ten.

Next to the picnic table, there was a bronze fountain, a sculpture of a family. There was a book in the child's lap, and the parents enveloped the child's body between their own. Emerging from the bronze book, like a pop-up card, were exquisite bronze birds in a birdbath, and the sound of the real water splashing over them made Mel smile. She carefully laid the books out on the table and examined each book individually. Three of them could fit into her pack; the other nine would need to be carried, which was fine. Mel liked the feel of the books in her arms as she walked to the bus stop. When the driver opened the door, Mel smiled up at him. She leaned against the front seat and rummaged through her pack, gathering the appropriate change. Once she'd deposited the fare, Mel sat down, but not without glancing at the other passengers and smiling – she couldn't help it – and then she carefully folded back the cover of *The Last Battle*.

When Mel got off the bus at her stop, she could hear Mr. Frohberger whistling. It was precise and clear, and it made her want to dance. She imagined being lifted into the air and twirled around and around. As she turned the corner, she spotted him sweeping the front walk.

"That's quite a load of books you've got there," he said.

"I picked up my library card today," Mel said, slowing her pace and then stopping. She shook her hair down onto her forehead, covering up the lump.

"So the library must have some good books."

"Thousands!" Mel answered. She could tell Mr. Frohberger would like to talk more, but she continually needed to lift a knee up to keep her books from slipping down and falling to the ground.

"You better keep moving before those books end up on the sidewalk."

"You're right. I probably should. Bye!" Mel started walking again.

"Give your grandmother my regards!"

"I will."

"Mr. Frohberger said to say hi," Mel called to Gladys, who was at her usual spot when Mel came through the door.

"Don't you be bothering Ed Frohberger."

"I wasn't . . . I was . . ."

"I told you, don't you be bothering Ed Frohberger. Cecily's caused him enough trouble."

Mel stood in purposeful silence with her books in her arms.

"And just make sure every last one of those books gets back to the library. The last thing I need is the police coming here looking for missing books!"

Mel almost laughed. *The police? Looking for missing library books?*

She walked to the couch and sat down, carefully putting the books on the floor beside her. She pulled the light blue library card from her pocket, turned it over, and read her signature, Melody Anastasia Tulley. Her head was throbbing. The card had not been all that easy to get, but it was worth it.

Mel thought about what Gladys had said, about Cecily causing Mr. Frohberger enough trouble, and she thought about Cecily saying that she wanted to apologize to him.

Mel knew what to expect the third morning, and she was awake and ready before Gladys came into the living room. Having folded back the tinfoil on the window when she woke up, Mel knew it was storming outside. As Gladys locked the door, Mel sat down in the corner with her plate of toast and looked up through the window into the dark clouds that filled the sky. She hadn't spoken to Gladys since last night. If Gladys could be cold, so could she.

The cracking thunder shook the glass in the window, and the tree branches scratched back and forth across the building's clapboard exterior.

Mel thought about the last storm, under the overpass. The towed Pinto, Cecily gone, and the long night she had spent curled up in a ball. A shiver ran up her spine. She set the plate and toast beside her on the floor and opened her book. The library wouldn't open for three hours. *Cecily will be back in twenty-three days.*

15

Sleeping Beauty

Although she'd snuck peeks at him on a number of occasions, this was the first time Mel had been so close. He was lying down, legs draped over the arm of the couch next to the window, asleep, or at least appearing to be asleep. Mel, unintentionally, took the extra moment his closed eyes afforded her to look at him longer than she would have if he were reading, or talking with a friend. She noticed his faded jean jacket, pressed white T-shirt, the way his hair hung in front of his face. He was definitely around her age, probably a little older.

"Can you believe it?" Marilyn said to Mel as she walked toward the sleeping teen.

Mel looked at the librarian and then at the boy on the couch. She felt her face blush, knowing full well she'd been caught staring.

"Come on. Wake up and help me with some of these books," Marilyn said.

The boy looked up.

Mel wanted to die. She could feel the heat on her face changing her skin from fair to flaming red.

"Hey," he said, nodding in her direction.

"Hey," Mel repeated.

"Melody," Marilyn said. "This is my son, Paul."

"Hi," Mel choked out.

"Paul, this is Melody. And believe it or not, when she comes to the library, she actually checks out books and reads them." The tone in Marilyn's voice was light and joking.

"Maybe *you* can convince him there's more to do in here than sleep," Marilyn said as she cast a smile in Mel's direction and then handed Paul an armload of books to shelve.

"Uh, I gotta go," Mel said, and then she headed for her usual table near the windows across from Paul, Marilyn, and the cart of unshelved books.

16

The Letter

The letter arrived exactly one week from the day Mel last saw Cecily.

Twenty days to go.

My Dearest Mel,

I'll bet you've read most of the books in the library by now. I know Gladys would have liked a little extra cash to help with groceries and things like that – don't worry about that. It will all work out. Don't let her make you feel guilty for asking for the library card. You made me so proud; I wanted to give you a standing ovation. And believe me I would have if my lawyer didn't give me strict orders to behave myself.

I loved it when the judge said you were important. You are important! You are the most important thing in my life! I wrote a list of all the things about you that make you so important to me. Here you go:

Because you are you, and I love you.

You are beautiful in all ways.
You are talented.
You are kind,
Intelligent,
Capable,
Loving,
Courageous and brave.
You are honest and you are wise,
Wiser than anyone I've ever known.
You are what fills my heart.

I know Gladys might tell you some awful things about me. I wish Tux was still alive because he would have opened the door and none of this would have happened. But nothing is going to change that now. I'm so sorry, Mel. Don't you worry, though. I'm going to make it up to you and we'll find a real home.

Love you forever.
White light,
Cecily

Mel brought the letter to her face. She could smell the smoke she knew Cecily had blown onto the paper before she sealed the envelope. "I love you, too, Cecily," she whispered, "more than anyone."

After folding the letter and sliding it back into the envelope, she tucked it into the front pocket of her backpack and went into the kitchen. She hoped that Gladys might ask her how Cecily was doing, that she might wonder if Cecily was okay. But Gladys didn't ask. She just glanced at Mel and went back to looking at the TV. The key had been moved; it was in front of the vacant chair at the table.

The next morning, Mel went by Frohberger's on her way to the library. She'd seen three or four greeting cards in cloudy plastic wrapping in the glass case by the cash register.

"What can I do for you this morning?" Mr. Frohberger asked.

"Um, I was wondering how much those cards are."

"How does fifty cents sound?" Mr. Frohberger said as he lifted them out of the case and put them on the counter.

Mel picked up the card with the sparkling birthday cake. "I'll take this one." She knew Cecily would love the glitter. "Do you have stamps?"

"No, sorry, I don't," Mr. Frohberger said as he shook his head. "But I'm sure the twenty-four-hour place down the street does."

"Okay," Mel said as she set two quarters down on the counter and carefully slipped the card into her pack.

She wanted to ask him more about when he knew her as a little girl, and about Tux, but Gladys's words about Cecily causing him enough trouble returned, and they kept her from asking.

Mel headed out the door for the bus. "I'll see you later," she called back.

17

Part-Time Job

"Mel, I'd like to talk to you," Marilyn said when Mel arrived at the library.

Although Mel couldn't imagine why Marilyn wanted to speak with her, she couldn't help but wonder if she were in trouble.

"Oh . . . sure," she replied, her mouth suddenly dry.

"The library is looking for a student to fill a part-time position. Just two hours, once a week, until the end of the summer. Is that something that you might be interested in applying for?"

"Oh . . . yes! Absolutely!" Both relief and surprise pulsed through Mel's veins.

"Well, then, here's a copy of the job posting."

Mel quickly read through the first few lines. "This sounds great, but I need to talk to my grandmother. Can I apply tomorrow?"

"We won't be hiring until next week; I just wanted to give you a heads-up. You're an ideal candidate: you seem to like books and you definitely know your way around the library!"

Looking again at the job posting, Mel could not believe her eyes. She quickly did the math: eight dollars and fifty cents an hour for two hours a week. That made seventeen dollars a week. Multiply that by the six weeks left in summer. Ten multiplied by six is sixty, and seven multiplied by six is forty-two. Forty-two and sixty make one hundred and two dollars – and it would be hers. She folded the piece of paper neatly in half and walked to a chair by the window, where she immediately opened it and proceeded to read and reread the job posting.

Children's Literacy Assistant: Saturdays. Mel definitely didn't have anything better to do on Saturdays. *Open to students aged 12 to 16.* Check. *Applicants should have a basic understanding with regards to how the library is set up.* Double check. *Enjoy reading.* Triple check. *Applications must be dropped off at the Circulation Desk.* No problem. *Remuneration is at eight dollars and fifty cents per hour.* Quadruple check. *Should funding be available in the fall, this position may be extended until December 31.* "Yes!" Mel said, and then she quickly looked around, realizing she'd spoken that *yes* out loud.

—

Perhaps the four-leaf clovers had been a sign. If Cecily were here, Cecily would have bought lottery tickets. There would have been vacation plans. Mel would have gone to the nearest library and learned the capitals of all the countries they'd visit, and they would have made lists of words and whole sentences in Spanish, French, or Italian.

Cecily would let the potential of winning linger, waiting for at least a week after the draw. The possibility that they would win only increased with each day they waited. As Mel grew older, she leaned on that possibility more and more until finally, she didn't want Cecily to buy lottery tickets. Because when Cecily did eventually check the ticket, and it wasn't a winner, she would spiral down, and Mel would be left trying to lift them both back up. Lottery lists always ended this way.

"But this is different," Mel said out loud as she walked toward Gladys's apartment. "This is real, and I've got a real chance at getting this job."

"There's a job for a student at the library," Mel said as she walked into the kitchen.

Gladys said nothing.

"The librarian said I should apply for it; she gave me the forms," Mel added.

"Well, I wouldn't be expecting that mother of yours

to be hanging around just because you've got a decent job. You'll probably just get started and then not be showing up." Gladys's eyes never left the TV.

"If I get the job," Mel said, and then paused. "I'll give you back the money for the things Cecily took." She hadn't planned to say that; it just came out.

"Well, from what I can see, you've got nothing but a bunch of rags for clothes." Gladys paused briefly and then continued. "You can't be expecting a person to hire someone who looks like they just crawled off the street."

Mel turned and walked back into the living room and sat on the couch. The truth was that she didn't need Gladys's permission.

18

Paul

"I can apply for the job," she told Marilyn the next day at the library.

"Wonderful. Believe me, it would be a good job for you. Here's an application form. Fill it out as best you can and bring it back in."

"Thanks," Mel said as she began to read the application. Then, looking back up, she smiled at Marilyn. "Thanks a lot."

Mel walked in the direction of her usual table, the words *believe me* repeated themselves over and over in her thoughts. They were words she didn't have a lot of faith in, but she'd try. She turned her attention again to the application form.

Looking down as she approached the table, she didn't notice Paul already sitting in one of the chairs.

"Hey," he said.

"Oh . . . I didn't see you." The words stumbled out of Mel's mouth.

Paul laughed. "Perfect. I was hoping to be invisible."

"No, I don't mean that. I can see you. I just didn't see you . . . because I was reading."

"Yeah, I know. I saw you coming. I'm just trying to look like I'm studying or my mom will have me shelving books for the rest of the afternoon."

Mel smiled.

"So, do you come here every day?" Paul asked.

"Uh, well, I'm staying with my grandmother for a month or so."

"Ah, summer vacation – me too. Well, I guess, if you can call this a summer vacation." Paul looked around the library, obviously unimpressed. "Do you want to play a game of chess?"

"Sure," Mel answered. She hadn't played since fourth grade when Mr. Russell, her teacher, taught the whole class.

Paul closed his books and hurried off toward the circulation desk. "I'll be right back."

Mel watched as Marilyn handed him the chess set. She purposely looked out the window as Paul turned, chessboard under his arm, and walked toward her. Mel could see that people were starting to congregate around the soup kitchen door.

Paul picked up both queens, one in each hand, placed

them behind his back, and then asked, "Left or right?"

"Left," Mel answered.

Pulling his hands from behind his back, palms open, Paul smiled and said, "Queen gets her color."

He reached across the table and set the white queen in front of her. It soon became obvious that Paul had played his fair share of chess. Hours passed like minutes, and neither of them spoke of anything unrelated to the game.

They didn't move when the loudspeaker came on: "Attention, patrons: The library will be closing in twenty minutes. Attention, patrons . . ."

"Paul, we've got to go." Marilyn said, interrupting the announcement. Both Mel and Paul looked up at her. "Do you need a lift home, Mel?"

"No, I'm good," Mel said as she got up to leave.

"Is this yours?" Paul asked, handing her the folded sheet he'd found under the chessboard.

"Are you sure you don't need a ride?" Marilyn asked again before Mel had a chance to answer Paul.

"Yes, I mean no . . . I mean . . . yes, that is my paper, and no, I'll take the bus. It stops about a block from my grandmother's."

"Thanks for the games," Paul said as he folded up the board and put it back in the box.

"Yeah, you too," Mel said as she handed the lid to Paul.

She should have left at the first closing call; the last bus that stopped near Frohberger's had left twenty minutes ago. But if she ran the first four blocks to Third Street, she'd be able to catch the 41 South bus. She'd have to walk a few extra blocks to get to Gladys's, but it would save her having to answer a thousand questions if Gladys somehow saw her getting out of a vehicle.

19

Mel's Letter

That night after Gladys went to bed, Mel pulled the greeting card she'd bought at Frohberger's out of the plastic wrapping and began to write.

Dear Cecily.

Then, carefully erasing the word *Cecily*, she wrote *Mom.*

Thanks for writing. Everything is good here, and Gladys and I are getting along just fine.

It wasn't the truth, but Mel knew she wasn't going to write about the scene in the kitchen, or about being lonely. Nor was she going to write about the whole thing with the key.

The library is great. I've been going almost every day.

She didn't mention Paul. Nor did she tell Cecily about the job possibility. It was better to wait until the job was hers.

I can't wait until you're out.

Then she erased the word *out* and replaced it with *back.*

Then we can find our own place. Only nineteen more days! I've been looking through the papers at the library, and there are lots and lots of places for rent.

Mel decided to tell Cecily about Fearless.

There's a kitten. He sleeps in the soup kitchen during the day. He's adorable! He needs a home. Maybe he could live with us. I love you and I miss you . . . like the flowers need the rain . . . Mel.

To the bottom of the card she added a P.S.

I bought this card from Frohberger's. Mr. Frohberger still runs the store.

Mel wanted to write that he remembered her, from when Mel was little, but she didn't. She hoped Cecily was still planning to apologize.

But right now, another truth was forming in Mel's mind. She knew she wouldn't have been at the table earlier in the day, with a library card, playing chess with Paul if Cecily hadn't been caught shoplifting. And today was a day she knew she'd treasure for a long time. The pendulum of Cecily Tulley, on which Mel spent her entire life, was swinging her from one extreme to another, yet again.

20

A Visit with Rose, Gus, and Fearless

Mel woke early the next morning and worked for hours on her application, answering all the questions as best she could. When she came to the part about references, she knew she could probably put Rose's name down, but she didn't have Rose's phone number or address. She didn't even know Rose's last name, for that matter. She decided to go by the soup kitchen. It would also give her a chance to visit with Fearless; she'd been missing him.

Mel had no sooner walked through the back door of the soup kitchen than Fearless spotted her. He jumped off the windowsill and pranced directly to her. Mel lifted him up and he leaned into her chest, pushing his cool nose against her cheek – all the while purring.

"You know Fearless doesn't give anybody but you that kind of love," Rose said, as she walked toward Mel.

Mel didn't respond. Instead she continued petting Fearless's silky black coat.

"I'm glad you came by; we've been wondering about you – hoping everything was okay." Rose glanced at Gus, who had come to join them.

"I'm good," Mel told them. "My mom sent me a letter." Mel didn't know why, but she wanted Rose to know that Cecily had written her. "We'll start looking for a place as soon as she's back. Only seventeen days!"

"Well, that's good," Rose said as she gently lifted one of Mel's curls off her forehead. "What happened here?"

"I fell," Mel said flatly, knowing that her voice probably lacked a sense of the truth. She looked down at Rose's bright pink canvas runners.

"Must have been quite a fall."

"I have a library card," Mel said, changing the subject. "I can check out fourteen books!"

"Well, I'd say that's just what you need," Rose said, giving a little wink. Then, with a more serious look, she glanced back at the bump on Mel's forehead.

"Yeah," Mel answered. She shook her hair back down over the bruise.

"So, what's that paper you're clinging to?" Rose asked.

"Well, I'm applying for a job at the library."

"What? Are you running that place already?" Rose teased. "I'd say you're a woman after my own heart."

"Ain't that the truth," Gus added. "Rose runs this

kitchen like a ship's captain. Got me workin' my knuckles to the bone peeling potatoes and whatnot."

"Speaking of which," Rose shot back, "could you peel a bag of carrots also?"

"Workin' me to the bone, Mel," Gus repeated, feigning pain and agony. "Let me know if they need anyone else; shelving books would be a dream job compared to this chain gang."

Mel laughed. "Okay, Gus," she said. "I will."

"So," Rose asked, "what exactly is the job?"

"It's just part-time, two hours a week," Mel said, "reading stories to preschoolers and stuff like that."

"Well, if you need a reference, you go right ahead and put my name down," Rose said as she wiped her hands on her apron.

"Actually, I was hoping that would be okay," Mel said and handed Rose the application form.

Rose wiped her hands once again on her apron before taking the sheet of paper from Mel. "I'd be honored to do this for you," she said.

"How about you sit down and sample this soup for me while I fill out the form?"

"Sounds like a fair trade to me," Mel joked.

Gus set a bowl and spoon in front of Mel and ladled out the thick colorful soup into her bowl.

Rose sat down on a stool and began filling out the form. Mel watched as Rose carefully wrote on each of the blanks. When Rose was done, she set the application form carefully on the counter and put her other hand on Mel's shoulder. "This is a good opportunity for you, but I don't doubt you've already figured that out."

"I know," Mel said. "Thanks."

"You're more than welcome. So tell me, what do you think about the soup?" Rose asked.

"It's great! What kind of soup is it?"

Gus and Rose stood side by side, smiling at her, and answered in unison, "Mulligatawny!"

"Quite a name, isn't it?" Gus added.

Mel left the soup kitchen and skipped to the library. Marilyn was at the desk when she walked in. Mel gave her the completed application form. Now came the hard part – waiting for an interview.

Rather than hang around the library, Mel decided to go back to the apartment. Gladys would be back from work by then, but Mel had plans to collect the empty bottles and cans that littered the tall grass around the back and sides of the building. Staying busy would keep her mind off the call for an interview, and she could turn the bottles and cans in for cash at Frohberger's. Gladys gave her an old pair of rubber gloves and two garbage bags.

"I'm going to deduct the cost of those bags off my rent," Gladys told her. "Years ago, when this building was owned by someone else, the property was something to be proud of – flower gardens, mowed lawn, trees pruned – but the new owners don't . . ."

Mel walked away as Gladys rambled on.

She cleaned for most of the afternoon. One bag she filled with cans and bottles, another with trash. More than one of the other tenants from the building thanked her as she worked.

"By the way," one guy said as he took a step toward her, "my name is Dave. So are you staying with your grandma now?"

"Mmm-hmm," Mel replied. She recognized him as the guy from down the hall, the one who Cecily had told to shut up. She turned away, looking for more garbage.

"I feel bad for her and everything, stuck in this building with a bunch of college students. This is no place for an old lady."

Mel threw the bag over her shoulder. The unexpected weight of it made her stumble.

Dave reached out to take the bag. "Here, let me help you," he offered.

"It's okay," Mel answered. "I've got it." With everything

she could muster, she hoisted the bag into the dumpster.

She then picked up the other filled bag, the one with the bottles and cans, and she headed to Frohberger's store. Altogether the recyclables were worth four dollars and twenty-five cents. Not much pay for an afternoon's work, but it was better than nothing.

Gladys met Mel at the door when she returned to the apartment. "What did that hoodlum want with you?"

"Oh, he was just thanking me for cleaning up the yard."

"You need to stay away from those boys. They're nothing but trouble."

"I will, Gladys," Mel answered – not because she knew they were trouble, but because she knew Gladys would not be convinced otherwise.

21

The Alley

By the next morning, Mel still hadn't heard back about an interview, and even though it was Gladys's day off and she could hang around the apartment, she decided to go to the library and check to make sure she hadn't missed the call.

It was startling to see police officers in the library. They were standing at the counter and speaking with Marilyn. Mel thought about her dream, the one she had in the car after fleeing from Craig's, the one about Cecily and the police. Weeks later, it still gave her the shivers.

She surveyed the library, hoping to spot Paul. At almost the same time that she located him, he looked up and smiled at her. He closed the textbook he was reading as Mel approached his table.

"So, is that English homework?" she asked, looking down at the book.

It seemed a little odd that Paul would be reading an English text in the summer.

"Yeah – sort of, anyway – summer school." There was nothing in the way Paul said the words *summer school* that gave any indication he enjoyed what he was doing.

"Summer school?" Mel lifted her eyebrows.

"Ah, well, let's just say that English is not my *best* subject."

"You'd think that with your mom being a librar –"

"I know," Paul interrupted. "But I suck at English. I'm doing this class for the second time. Anyway, whatever. I've got three weeks until I finish this course, and then I can go back to having a life again."

"Oh, that'll be good," Mel said, but she was disappointed. Paul would not be sticking around the library once the course was finished.

"Maybe I can help," she offered.

"Can you make sense of poetry?"

"Some." It was a lie. She loved poetry.

"Okay, so what do you figure this means?" Paul opened his textbook and started to read the poem out loud.

Two or three words into the poem, Paul stopped reading and pushed the textbook in her direction. "You should probably just read this yourself."

Mel turned the book so that it faced her, and set her hand on the page. She read the title, "Flying," gave it a momentary thought, and then began reading the poem out loud.

"Okay. I guess I should have known," Paul told her when she finished.

"Known what?"

"I should have known this would be a breeze for you."

"Really?"

"Well, for one, you smiled the whole time you read that poem, and two, you do seem to check out more books than anyone else around here."

"I've just always liked books."

Paul laughed. "I can't imagine ever liking books. I've always hated them. Well, not books, so much. I mean . . . whatever."

"I think this poem is about what someone will do to follow their dreams, about overcoming a fear of looking silly or foolish," Mel said, picking up the book and rereading the poem silently.

"You know what? I don't need to hand this in until tomorrow," Paul said.

"I don't mind helping you with it."

"No, it's fine. And anyway – even if I fail the poetry part of this course, I think I've passed the rest. After all, this is the second time I've done English this year. Besides, there is something I want to show you." Paul took the textbook from Mel and motioned for her to follow him.

She noticed the title on his English book and the number eight. Paul must be in eighth grade, going into ninth – a year ahead of her. He stacked his books and put them on the floor beside the table.

"So, what do you want to show me?" Mel asked.

"Well, did you see the cops when you came in?" Paul asked as he started to walk.

"Yeah, why?"

"Well, we found a homeless guy half dead on the steps when we got here this morning."

"So, you called the cops?"

"Well, first my mom called the ambulance, but the cops came, too."

Mel wondered what it was that Paul was planning to show her as they entered a long, narrow hallway. At the end of the hallway, there was an exit light, with glowing red letters, hanging over the door.

"The fire department arrived first," Paul said as he looked back at her. "Anyway, I'm pretty sure the guy we found on the steps lives here in the alley. I see him every day. He lines up at the soup kitchen and then walks back into the alley when he's done."

Mel felt uneasy; Paul was definitely the person she'd seen in the window.

"I'm just kind of curious. Aren't you?"

Mel didn't answer.

When they got to the end of the hall, Paul pushed on the door and held it for Mel to walk through. He then picked up a small stone from the ground, and lodged it in the hinge of the door, leaving it slightly ajar.

"I'm not sure this is such a good idea," Mel said as she looked down the alley.

It was narrow and shadowed by the brick building that towered next to it. Mel knew from experience that this type of alley was not the kind you explored for fun.

"Nah, it's fine," Paul said as he set off at a brisk pace. "Come on. It's daylight. We're fine."

Yeah, right, Mel thought as she followed him. *What would you know about alleys and whether or not they're safe?* She was definitely going against her better judgment.

"You see all this stuff?" Paul asked her.

"Yeah, so?" Mel said nonchalantly.

She wondered if Paul was planning on ransacking the makeshift lean-to that was built against the chain-link fence – even though it soon became clear that someone had already done that. All the contents of a shopping cart were strewn into the adjacent empty parking spot, including collections of cans in large plastic onion sacks. The whole scene gave Mel an uneasy feeling. A blackened aluminum pot, a makeshift fire pit, bits and pieces of garbage, and an old sleeping bag on top of three or four layers of flattened cardboard were in a disheveled heap next to the fence. The only thing left intact seemed to be the newspaper and some plastic florescent pink flagging woven into the small diamonds of the chain link. The dark stains on the concrete nearby were most likely from the shattered green bottle – most of its contents mixed with dirt in a dried puddle. Paper napkins, stained with what Mel imagined was blood, sat among various empty brown paper bags.

Paul moved the bottles, papers, and clothes around with his foot. "I've watched him wander in and out of this alley tons of times. See that window?"

Mel looked in the direction of the window.

"It looks directly into the alleyway." Paul pointed down the alley toward the street.

It reminded Mel of that first time she and Cecily had lined up at the soup kitchen.

"Man, I can't believe people can live like this," Paul said as he kicked around the cup and pot. He righted the beaten-up shopping cart and raised his foot to the handle.

"Don't do that!" Mel shouted at Paul.

"Do what?"

"Don't trash that cart!

"Whoa! Sorry! You don't need to get all excited. I was just going to give it a little push." Paul cast a surprised look at Mel.

"These are someone's things," Mel said as she bent down. She was annoyed with his arrogance and she meant for him to know it.

What had caught her eye was a small purple sack with the words "Crown Royal" embroidered into the fabric. It was poking out from the sleeping bag. Mel knew that it had to be important if it was being stowed in the worn sleeping bag. She moved in closer and picked it up. She loosened the drawstring. Inside was a collection of shells. Most were broken, as was the plastic face of the Westclox pocket watch. There was also a set of playing cards wrapped together with a bunch of rubber bands, and part of a photograph tucked in on top of the cards. Mel knew that what she was doing was, in some ways, snooping. But she also knew that if there was any chance of finding out who these things belonged to, she would need to look; a part of her wondered if maybe these things belonged to Gus.

"What's that?" Paul asked.

"Just some shells, a watch, an old photograph and . . ."

"What kind of shells?"

"Seashells," Mel said.

"So, what are you going to do with all that stuff?" Paul asked in a conciliatory manner.

"Oh, I don't know. I was thinking that I should take it to the police station." What she actually planned to do was take the small bag to Rose; she might know to whom it belonged.

Mel looked down the alley. "You know, we should probably get out of here."

"What's the hurry?"

"Those guys," Mel said. She gestured with her head, toward the street. It was the way that one of the guys moved as he walked; it reminded her of Craig's walk. Fear raced down her limbs, telling her to get out of here. It made no sense. Mel was sure Craig didn't know about Gladys. Cecily always told people that it was just her and Mel.

"Ah, good idea," Paul said.

When Mel and Paul reached the door into the library, they found it locked. Either someone had discovered it open, or the rock that Paul had set in the hinge had become dislodged. Paul pulled on the door again, hoping it would open. Mel looked back down the alley, then quickly headed into the street and around the corner to the front of the library.

"Do you know those guys?" Paul asked, chasing after her.

"No," Mel answered, "I don't, but I've gotta go. My grandmother is expecting me."

Mel left Paul standing on the library steps and ran as fast as she could. She sped down four blocks and then circled back to the alley behind the soup kitchen to be sure there was some distance between her and the guy who reminded her of Craig. *Cecily would be back in fifteen days.*

Rose was surprised, but glad, to see Mel again so soon.

"You look like you just bumped into death or something. What's going on?" Rose asked.

"No, I'm fine. I just found this by the library. I think it belongs to a guy that was beaten up last night. He's in the hospital. I thought you might know him. I'm hoping that it wasn't Gus."

Rose looked at the small purple bag, pulled the top open, and nodded. "Gus is here; you don't need to worry about him. But I'll check with him," she said. "If it's Carl's, Gus will return it to him."

"Thanks, Rose. I've gotta go."

"Hey, what about that job?" Rose called out as Mel turned to leave.

"No interview yet, but cross your fingers!"

"Okay, but take some of these with you," Rose said as she reached for a couple of homemade cookies and handed them to Mel.

"Thanks, Rose." Mel took a bite of one, and headed back out the door to the alley.

As she walked to Gladys's, Mel tried not to think about the guy that had walked like Craig. But the more she tried not to, the more she started to believe that it was Craig. She decided that from now on, she would catch her bus at the next stop, a block and a bit away from the library and the soup kitchen.

"Where have you been?" Gladys asked sternly from the kitchen when Mel opened the apartment door. It was unusual for Gladys to say anything when Mel arrived.

"At the library," Mel said, catching her breath.

"So, where are your books?"

"Ah – I didn't check anything out. I still have something I'm reading."

"I don't see any reason for you to be going to the library if you don't need any books. You better not be getting into trouble. Your supper is cold and you'll have to eat it that way; I waited forty-five minutes for you to get here."

Mel was shocked. Gladys never waited for her.

"What? You're standing there like some stone statue. Sit down."

Gladys also never planned dinner. Usually she left a

small plate of food on the coffee table if Mel wasn't home when Gladys made dinner. It wasn't as if meals arrived at any particular time. From what Mel could tell, food arrived when Gladys was hungry, or felt like cooking. There didn't seem to be any rule about having to eat at the table, or against eating in front of the TV – or while sitting on the couch, for that matter.

On the few occasions she had taken her plate from the coffee table and walked into the kitchen where Gladys was, Gladys's eyes had remained glued to the TV. But tonight Mel sat at the little red arborite table and Gladys sat across from her. The TV was off, and the key sat in the center of the table between them. Mel noticed Gladys shifting uncomfortably in her chair.

Finally, when Mel had almost finished eating, Gladys spoke up. "So, I heard some bum was found bleeding all over the front steps of the library this morning."

Mel looked up from her plate.

"I guess for once I'm not wondering if it's you or Cecily."

"Cecily and I were never bums," Mel said as she picked up her plate and went to the sink, purposely turning away from Gladys.

"I didn't mean that," Gladys answered back. "I just meant . . ." Gladys stopped.

Mel turned on the water in the sink, washed her plate, and stacked the dish, leaving what Gladys had to say unspoken.

After Mel dried her hands, she returned to the living room and curled up under her blanket. She looked around at the walls, the small woven carpet under the coffee table, and the locks on the doors. Then she opened her book and began to read.

22

The Phone Call

Today was different; Gladys was going shopping. Instead of toast for breakfast, there was a freezer-burnt store-bought blueberry muffin, a small knife, and a dab of margarine.

"Here," Gladys said when Mel sat down at the table.

Mel looked at the muffin. It made her think about Cecily and their last visit to the bakery.

"Well, you'll need to get eating if you're going to finish that before I'm on my way," Gladys said, interrupting Mel's thoughts. Gladys glanced at the key still sitting on the table.

Mel took a bite of the muffin.

Gladys drew in a stiff breath and then began to busy herself: writing her list, gathering up cloth sacs for her groceries, and cutting the last of the coupons from the flyer that had come in the mail the day before.

When Mel finished her muffin, she picked up her pack, books, and flip-flops, and walked out the door.

Gladys had no sooner locked the door behind them than the phone started ringing – and the phone never rang. Mel knew it was the library calling about an interview. Gladys appeared not to notice.

"It's the phone!" Mel blurted out. Gladys stopped and looked at Mel. "The phone – it's ringing! And I know it's the library calling me about an interview!"

"I've got to go or I'll miss my bus," Gladys said in a matter-of-fact voice.

"Please," Mel pleaded.

Gladys gave a sigh and unlocked the door. Mel ran for the phone.

"Hello, yes, this is Melody." Mel smiled at Gladys and mouthed the words *It's the library*.

Gladys's face remained stern as she lifted her key and made a locking motion. Mel nodded. Gladys turned as though leaving, unaware that Mel could see that Gladys had only taken one step before stopping momentarily and then continuing through the hall and down the stairs.

An interview – tomorrow – ten-thirty. Mel placed the words in her memory. She hung up the phone and bounced toward the open door. The top lock could be locked from the inside, by setting it and pulling the door shut. Mel smiled; she could leave the key on the table.

As Mel ran down the stairs, she was barely able to

142 THE PHONE CALL

contain the excitement bubbling out of her. She practically leaped across the street to the store to tell Mr. Frohberger the good news.

"Well, I'd say you're having a mighty fine day," Mr. Frohberger said as Mel bounded in.

"I am. I've got an interview at the library tomorrow!"

She hadn't mentioned the possibility of a job to Mr. Frohberger, but now it seemed so close it was almost real, and she wanted to tell someone.

"It's just an interview, but maybe, if I'm lucky, I'll get the job."

"Oh, I'd say that if they hire *you* that *they're* the lucky ones. So is this your first job interview?"

"Mmm-hmm."

"Well, you'll have to get ready for it." Mr. Frohberger was very businesslike. "Be prepared to answer some tough questions."

"Really?"

"Oh, for sure. That's a good job there, working at the library."

"Like, what kind of questions?" Mel was feeling a bit nervous.

"Oh, you know, questions about your experience. What you're good at. Things like that."

"Okay," Mel said, nodding her head. "Well, I don't

have any experience. I've never had a job. But I can sing, and I do like to read."

"Sounds great. So, what do you have planned for the rest of the day?"

"Nothing, really."

"Well, if you'd like, you could help me clean, stock, and organize the shelves. That'll give you a little work experience."

"Sure, that sounds like fun!"

Mr. Frohberger used a moving dolly to bring out boxes of canned goods from the back, and Mel took a damp cloth and dusted all the shelves. She then restocked them, making sure to turn each product's label toward the aisle. Mr. Frohberger called it "facing the shelves." Mel thought the freshened "faces" looked rather pretty.

Mel had just finished positioning the last of the cans of soup when Mr. Frohberger came down from his upstairs suite with cucumber sandwiches and suggested to Mel that she get them each a root beer out of the cooler. They were sitting down on the front steps and eating their sandwiches when Gladys came around the corner.

Mel almost choked on her root beer. "I've got an interview," she blurted out. "Tomorrow . . . ten-thirty."

"Hello, Ed," Gladys said, ignoring Mel.

Mr. Frohberger picked up on Gladys's apparent disapproval. "Good afternoon, Gladys. Your granddaughter here has been a big help in the store today."

"That's good; I would hope she has not been a nuisance. Melody, I'll need you to help me bring these bags up the stairs. Good day, Ed."

Mel took the last bite of her sandwich, thanked Mr. Frohberger, and set off down the street, carrying the three bags that Gladys had left on the sidewalk. One, Mel noticed, was lighter than the other two. Inside was a clear plastic bag wrapped around a white shirt on a hanger.

Mel delivered the bags to the kitchen and skipped into the living room to the place on the shelf where she kept her things. There weren't many clothes to choose from, but what she did have was clean. She picked out her orange T-shirt and best jeans. Her only shoes were well worn, stained, and tight on her feet. If only she could buy a new pair, but there was no chance of that. She took the beaten-up runners into the bathtub with her, and filled the grand old tub to the brim. With the nailbrush and some hand soap, she did what she could to get them – and herself – clean.

Gladys was walking into the living room when Mel came out of the bathroom. "You can have that blouse," Gladys said, pointing to the white shirt in the clear plastic dry-cleaning bag on the couch. "It was left at the shop for over a year, and we have a policy about leaving things at the dry-cleaners. I'm sure whoever it belonged to has long since outgrown it."

Mel picked up the hanger and lifted it up so she could see the shirt. She read the tag clipped to the top of the plastic: Fan's Dry-Cleaning. The white blouse, with its – one, two, three, four, five, six, seven, eight, nine, ten, eleven, twelve, thirteen, fourteen, fifteen, sixteen – tiny white buttons was beautiful. It looked brand new. Mel loved it. "It's gorgeous," Mel said as she walked into the kitchen.

Gladys remained silent, her gaze on the TV. Then out of the corner of her eyes, Mel saw it. A shiny new brass key set next to the one she'd given back to Gladys.

"I love the shirt, Gladys," Mel said. "Thank you."

"Well, don't be taking it out of the plastic until you need to."

23

The Interview

The office for the children's librarian was at the back of the library, next to the picture book collection and just opposite and around a corner to what Mel now knew to be the back exit.

Although the louvered blinds on the window to the office were turned down slightly, Mel could see a woman speaking to someone about Mel's age, maybe a little older. Above the woman's desk was a framed poster of the book *The Mysteries of Harris Burdick*. Mel took this as a good omen; it was one of her all-time favorite books. She sat down at a small round table with her back to the window. She looked down at her faded jeans and shoes. If the canvas had dried, the shoes might have been white, or at least whiter, but soaking wet they were gray and dirty-looking. Mel had put toilet paper in her shoes, to stop the ridiculous suctioning noise they belched out with each step she took. A corner of the tissue was sticking out of one shoe, and she quickly tucked it back in.

As the door to the office opened, Mel heard the woman thank the girl for coming in. Mel's palms began to sweat and the patch of dry skin on the back of her knee began to itch.

"Think *calm*," she whispered to herself.

"Miss Tulley?" The woman who was doing the interviewing peered around the corner in Mel's direction.

"Hi," Mel said. She was sure there was a more appropriate way to greet someone who was about to interview you, but the only other thing she could think to say was "Your Honor."

"Please, come in and sit down," the woman said.

Mel stepped lightly, almost tiptoeing, as she took her first steps toward the office door. And although her shoes didn't squelch, she felt her face heat up as the woman's eyes traveled past her new white blouse to her gray canvas runners.

"They're wet," Mel said as she stepped into the office. She sat down, crossed her ankles, and tucked her feet under the chair.

"Not to worry. This carpet has seen a whole lot worse than water," the woman said. Then she smiled and reached out her hand to shake Mel's. "My name is Lisa."

"Hi," Mel said. "I guess you already know, but my name is Melody Tulley. I go by Mel."

"It's nice to meet you, Mel. Let's get started. I've read through your application and I want to tell you that it's apparent you put a lot of thought into answering the questions. I especially liked how you answered the question about who your favorite author is and why. I also have more than one favorite, but Chris van Allsburg is definitely on my top-ten list."

The librarian pointed to the framed poster. Mel noted the signature. Lisa paused for a moment; Mel knew that Lisa was giving her a chance to say something if she wanted, but she wasn't sure what to say.

"Do you have any experience working with children?"

"Not really," Mel answered. "But I do like kids and I have helped out with cleaning and stocking in the store across the street from my grandmother's – I didn't get paid or anything, but I guess that's not really experience working with children, is it?"

Mel felt a bit awkward for mentioning the part about cleaning and stocking shelves when there was absolutely no connection between working with children and helping out at Frohberger's.

"That's fine. Volunteer work experience is good. Okay, how about with speaking in front of people? I know you are only twelve, and I don't expect you to have a lot of experience, but any experience at all – maybe something in school, or church?"

"Well . . ." Mel thought about all the days she and Cecily spent busking on street corners. She remembered a Christmas Eve in a shelter. After dinner, the volunteers at the shelter set up a talent show. Mel sang "Silent Night" and Cecily played the guitar. Later Mel recited *The Night Before Christmas*. The talent show went on into the night. No one wanted it to end.

"I have sung in front of people and recited poetry," Mel answered.

"Oh, that sounds great. Where did you do that?" Lisa asked.

"Uh," Mel paused, "in a church basement on Christmas Eve."

Mel knew this sounded like she was with her family at church, all proper and everything, but sometimes, Mel knew, a part-truth was better than the whole truth.

"Well, if you can do that, I am sure that you won't have any trouble reading stories during our preschool storytime."

It was starting to sound like Mel might be offered the job.

"One last question, Mel. If we offered you the job, could you start tomorrow?"

Mel didn't need to think about when she would start. Her mind was racing. She'd start today, right now, whenever they wanted her to start. "Yes, I could."

"Great. Do you have any questions about the position?"

"Not really," Mel said. But what she had actually wanted to say was that she wanted the job more than anything, and that she was sure she could do it. But those weren't questions, and it seemed she couldn't come up with one that would get her message across.

"It's been a pleasure to meet you, Mel. Thanks for coming in. I'll be making a decision before the end of the day."

"You're welcome," Mel said as she stood up to leave.

Glancing through the glass, Mel saw another girl, about the same age as Mel, with a woman who acted like she must be the girl's mother, sitting at the table. Mel let her fingertips run down the buttons on her blouse. She wiped her sweaty palms on her jeans and gave her runners a quick disappointed glance as she moved through the doorway.

"Miss Beauvais?" Lisa asked. "Please come in."

Both people stood and walked toward the door. Miss Beauvais, Mel noted, had perfectly straight hair. And it was pinned with a barrette in the exact spot that Miss

Beauvais probably wanted it to be. It wasn't anything like Mel's unruly hair. Mel's hair did what it wanted, when it wanted, however it wanted. Miss Beauvais's long hair sat still; it hung down her back like a smooth and silky blanket and stopped with a flawless straight line and a slight tuck. And the word "Beauvais" – of all the names a person could have. "Beauvais" was a word Mel knew. It was an incredibly beautiful Gothic cathedral in France, the Beauvais Cathedral. She and Cecily dreamed about visiting it when they made it big and toured Europe.

Mel hung around the library long enough to see Miss Beauvais and her mother leave. No one else appeared, and Mel noted that her chances were probably one in three. Normally she was an optimist, but she was also a realist, and something about Miss Beauvais and her mother, and the way they appeared so perfect, was getting the best of her. *Probably*, Mel thought, *Miss whoever-she-is Beauvais will get the job*.

Mel had just finished checking out a stack of books, one of which included a photograph of the Beauvais Cathedral, when Lisa tapped her on the shoulder.

"Could I speak with you in my office?" she asked.

"Sure." Mel turned, her arms full with books, and walked just behind Lisa as they returned to her office.

Lisa offered her a seat, but when Mel sat down, the stack of books almost reached her chin. She felt silly and childlike.

"I'd like to offer you the job. I think you'd be perfect!" It was almost more than Mel could accept – someone using the word "perfect" with regards to her. Miss Beauvais, it had seemed to Mel, held all the qualities of "perfect," and although a small voice inside of Mel whispered that this job offer just might be too good to be true, Mel quieted it and let her lungs fill with a mixture of pride and pure joy.

"Can you be here tomorrow?" Lisa asked.

"Absolutely!"

"Fantastic! Come in at nine and we'll do the first session together. I'll have a name tag at the front desk for you, and a blue vest. You can pick them up when you sign in tomorrow."

A name tag, a vest, and a real job. Mel could hardly contain the excitement racing around inside of her.

One hundred and two dollars, one hundred and two dollars, one hundred and two dollars. Mel repeated the number over and over in her head all the way to Gladys's.

Cecily would be back in thirteen days. And then a sudden realization caught Mel in the back: *What if Cecily didn't want to stay in Riverview?* Mel pushed that thought aside. Cecily had said there was no going back to Craig's, and Mel wanted to believe her – and there wasn't really anywhere else to go, at least not right away.

Mr. Frohberger was looking out the front window of the store, as he often seemed to do, when Mel walked by. Sometimes she wondered if he waited by the window each time the bus stopped on Thirty-Seventh, hoping someone he knew would get off the bus. For Mel, walking up the front steps into Frohberger's was like coming home. Mr. Frohberger would ask about her day and listen to her stories. Today was no different.

"Well, that's about the best news I've heard all week," he exclaimed when she told him she'd gotten the job.

Mel reenacted the story about her runners belching and squelching as she desperately tried to walk quietly into the library for her interview. She pulled the soggy toilet paper from her shoes and they both laughed so hard that they cried.

"Gladys will be proud of you," Mr. Frohberger said as Mel turned to leave the store.

Mel didn't quite know what to say, and so she said the truth. "I hope so."

—

"I got the job," Mel said as she walked into the kitchen. "I start tomorrow. I'll be able to give you the money Cecily owes you."

Gladys said nothing at first. Mel noticed that a small triangle of tinfoil was folded over in the kitchen window, giving Gladys a clear view of the street below and of Frohberger's.

Mel was about to return to the living room when Gladys spoke. "You hang on to your wages. That's your money."

24

The First Saturday

Marilyn greeted Mel as she came in the front door of the library.

"I suspect this is for you," she said as she held up the vest.

Mel took note of the name tag pinned on the front – "Riverview Public Library Staff," and below that, her name, "Melody." Her name tag and her vest and – better than anything – her job. The only thing that could have made the moment better was if Cecily had been there to share it with her.

As Mel walked over to the children's storytime area, the voice that had yesterday whispered the job offer might be too good to be true was at last silenced.

Lisa was busy preparing for the kids.

"Can I do anything to help?" Mel asked.

"You could set these cushions out in a semicircle. Then we'll sit down and talk a bit before the crowds arrive."

"Crowds?" Mel asked.

"Just kidding. Eight, maybe ten kids," Lisa said as she smiled.

Mel picked up the pile of cushions and set each down on the floor in front of the small chair. Parents and children started to arrive – most seemed to be seasoned veterans of the library storytime.

After a few minutes, Lisa nodded to Mel and then quieted the waiting children. "I want to welcome all of you to our preschool storytime this week. As you can see, we have a special person with us. Please join me in welcoming Melody, our summer student, to storytime."

The nine little kids, all sitting on their parents' laps in a semicircle facing Mel and Lisa, clapped wildly. Lisa sat down on the small red chair, gestured to Mel to sit down on the carpet, and she read the first story. Mel noted how Lisa held the book up, how she talked about the picture on the cover and the title, how she asked the kids if they'd read the book. All the kids had stories and all too soon it was Mel's turn to read a book.

This, Mel thought, *is not as easy as it looks*. First, there was reading upside down, since she had to hold the book open in front of the kids and look down from the top of the page. Then it was her suddenly dry lips sticking to her front teeth, and then the words to *Brown Bear, Brown Bear*, which seemed to catch between her tongue and the roof of her mouth. The back of her knee was itching, her face was sweating, and all the little kids were staring and waiting for her to continue reading.

Lisa brought her a glass of water.

"Here," she said. "Have a sip."

Mel took a drink and continued. Somewhere between the words "Blue horse, blue horse" and the following page, the kids started reading with her, and then it was fun.

"You're a natural," Lisa told her later when the children had gone. "Here is a list of books for next week's storytime. Most of them should be on the shelf. If you'd like, you can take them home and read them ahead of time."

Mel methodically went through the shelves, finding all but one of the books on the list. After checking them out under the staff account, she carefully put as many books as she could into her pack, tucked the others under her arm, and headed for the bus stop.

She thought back to when she first fell in love with books, and with that thought and this being the first day of her first real job, she missed Cecily. Mel could never remember a time when they'd been separated for so long. The twelve days until Cecily's return felt like forever, but there was also a part of her that was nervous. Cecily liked change.

25

Tux

Mr. Frohberger was sitting on the front steps of the store, drinking a soda, when Mel came around the corner.

"So, how'd your first day on the job go?" he asked.

"Well, I was pretty nervous at first, but I think it went okay."

"Would you like a lemon-lime soda or a root beer?"

Mel was thirsty and she wanted one, but she also felt a little guilty. She didn't have the extra money to be buying pop, and she also knew she shouldn't always accept free ones from Mr. Frohberger.

"No, thanks."

"Are you sure? Because the cooler is full and today is your first day on the job."

"Oh, okay."

"Then go ahead and pick one out for yourself," Mr. Frohberger said. "I'm going to enjoy a bit more of this sunshine before it disappears behind the clouds.

Mel set her armload of books and her backpack next

to Mr. Frohberger and climbed the concrete steps that led into the old store. She liked that he trusted her not to steal anything. But she also noted how easy it would be; he was sitting outside, he'd never know. She took a long look at the neat row of colorful chocolate bars – her eyes settled on a box of Oh Henry!, her favorite.

Mr. Frohberger's whistling caught her off guard, but it also reminded her that she did not want to steal from him, nor – for that matter – from anyone else ever again. Mel lifted a root beer from the cooler, opened it on the old-fashioned metal bottle opener that hung on the wall by the door, and went back outside.

As she sat next to Mr. Frohberger, the time seemed right, so Mel posed the question she'd been dying to ask him.

"Would you tell me more about Tux?"

She didn't ask if he'd tell her more about herself when she was little. That seemed kind of silly, but she hoped he would.

Mr. Frohberger's face shifted. "Like I told you before, he and I were good friends. In fact, we sat on these very steps and drank more than a few ice-cold root beers together. He was a good man."

"Gladys never talks about him," Mel said, wanting Mr. Frohberger to continue.

"Hmm, well, it's hard sometimes to talk about our loved ones when they're gone. I don't doubt she misses him; Tux was pretty much all Gladys had, at least until you came back. What do you want to know?"

"Everything. I don't really know anything about him."

"Well, isn't that a shame," Mr. Frohberger said. "I remember the first day you came in here. I watched you as you walked down the aisle, taking the whole place in, not missing a thing. I saw you stop in front of the curtains at the back of the store and look at them for a while. When you told me your grandmother was Gladys, I just presumed you knew."

"Knew what?" Mel was almost afraid to ask.

"Well, that you remembered Tux, knew that he performed his magic act on the stage behind those curtains. But then, I guess, that was before you were born."

"Cecily told me about the magic shows, but I don't remember the magic," Mel said, and she felt the huge gaping hole deep inside of her. It was a place between her ribs and her stomach, and it made her sad.

"You couldn't have been more than about two and a half, three maybe, when Cecily . . . well, when . . . you left. Let's see. One thing your Grandpa Tux loved to do was pull a bouquet of bright orange flowers out from behind your ear; in fact, he used to make you giggle every time he did that trick."

Mel tried, but no matter how deep she dug, she couldn't remember.

"Heck, I once saw him dangle a blank piece of paper from the ceiling. He had a volunteer from the audience write a number between one and one hundred on a different piece of paper, and then he told that volunteer to show the number to the person next to them, and then – believe it or not – with a flick of the wrist that number was written on the paper dangling from the ceiling. All with the wave of a handkerchief! I never could figure that one out," Mr. Frohberger said, shaking his head and smiling. "Over the years, he pulled everything from doves to chocolate bars out of nowhere."

All the words found their way into the place inside of Mel that was hurting. They layered themselves over one another. The words didn't fill the void, but they made it better. It was the feeling a warm scarf gives your neck on a cold day; it was comforting.

"Cecily . . ." Mel stopped. She was going to say that Cecily could pull a coin out from behind an ear, but she didn't.

"My wife, Betty, she's passed on now, fourteen years ago this September. She was a singer. Mostly she just warmed up the audience for Tux. Your grandfather was the big draw. We'd have chairs set up right down the aisle, practically out the front door some Saturdays."

Mel could feel a sweet sense of pride stirring within her.

"Those matinees sure were popular, and not just for the kids – it was quite a show, complete with penny prizes. All the neighborhood kids wanted to be magicians, but the only one who learned all that sleight of hand was . . . well . . . *that* Cecily."

Mel looked down at the concrete steps. For the first time, she felt uneasy with Mr. Frohberger. It was the way she felt whenever anyone said anything bad about Cecily. It wasn't that what he said was bad, it was just the way he emphasized the word "that."

"You remind me of Tux," Mr. Frohberger said.

"I do?" Mel couldn't help but smile. She took a drink of her root beer and let the fizz bubble around in her mouth.

"You always did. Quick to share a smile – both of you."

Mel kept listening. His tone was not so much serious but something else – she could tell that he thought Tux was special.

"There was something about Tux; he had a way that

put people at ease. He was honest and hardworking." Mr. Frohberger paused. It wasn't the kind of pause you make when you are leaving room for someone to respond to what you said. It was the kind of pause you take when you are thinking about what you've just said, and letting the feelings that thought brings sit with you awhile.

"He never gave up on people. There was the time when the new all-night chain stores came into town. I almost lost this place. It was Tux's idea to do the Saturday Magic Matinees, pull people in. It kept me in business."

Mel didn't want Mr. Frohberger to stop talking, but she sensed that he was about to. "Did he ever bring me here?"

"Oh yes, he brought you here all the time. You took your first steps on the worn-out floors of this old store."

"I did?"

"You sure did, and I think you might have eaten your first bit of chocolate here also. If I'm not mistaken, I think it was an Oh Henry!"

Mel felt her face blush with the guilt that she'd even considered for a moment how easy it would be to steal from Mr. Frohberger.

"Tux used to sit you up on the counter and he and I would shoot the breeze. Mind you, once you figured out how to walk, well – you would run, full speed up and down the aisle, pulling things off the shelves. Tux would be chasing you and you'd be squealing. Those were good days."

Mel waited, hoping that Mr. Frohberger would go on. "I wish I remembered him." The words left her lips before she realized that she was saying them out loud.

Mr. Frohberger looked directly into Mel's eyes. "I'm sure you've got a memory of Tux somewhere inside, Mel; you just haven't found it yet, but it's there. I'm sure it is."

A man and his son came around the corner and walked up the steps and into the store. Mr. Frohberger called out that he'd be right with them.

He set his hand on Mel's shoulder as he stood up. "Want me to take that empty bottle?"

"Sure, thanks," Mel said.

Mr. Frohberger smiled back at her. "My pleasure."

Back at the apartment, Mel looked at Gladys and thought about her and Tux and Cecily and about how they had once been a family. It was hard to imagine Gladys loving anyone.

"Mr. Frohberger was saying –"

"I thought I told you not to be bothering Ed Frohberger."

It was true Gladys had told her this before; what was

different was that this time Gladys didn't sound as angry.

"He just –"

"I said to leave *him* alone," Gladys interrupted.

But Mel had started asking about her past and now she knew she wasn't going to stop. Her need to know was greater than her fear of Gladys. "I just wanted to know about Tux. I wanted to know how he died. I just wanted to know about . . ." Mel stopped. Her gut was twisting. It seemed like forever before Gladys said anything.

"I'll tell you this," Gladys said, without looking at Mel. "He died a broken man with a broken heart, and your mother is to blame for that!"

The words shut Mel down and they stung like salt on an open wound, leaving her sick, as though she were about to vomit. Mel walked to the living room, vowing to never ask again. She sat down on the couch and began a list of things she and Cecily would need. She'd take her one hundred and two dollars and buy things for their apartment.

Dishes.
A chili-pepper apron like Rose's.
A cat dish.
One pot. One frying pan.
Forks, knives, spoons, three cups, a teapot.

Sheets, two beds, pillows, and blankets.

Mel looked up from her list and into the living room.

Curtains, curtains for our windows.
Windows that open.
Birds that sing.
Sunshine.
Singing and laughter.
Cecily.
Me.
And friends visiting.

Tomorrow would be eleven days. It felt like an eternity.

26

A Date

Mel hadn't seen Paul in four days. She felt guilty, but she'd been busy: a day spent filling in the application, a day at Frohberger's, the interview, and then the first Saturday.

"So I saw those guys again, the ones who were in the alley that day," Paul said as he opened the front door of the library.

Mel wanted to ask if he'd seen them in the library, or if he'd overheard them talking about her. But she didn't. "Yeah, well, next time you go into the alley, take one of your other friends."

"Well, *actually*, I don't have any other friends in Riverview. Basically – you're it."

Mel stopped and turned to face Paul. "What do you mean, you 'don't have any other friends'?"

"I'm just here for the summer, as part of the custody agreement.

I was supposed to be signed up for a sports camp, but seeing as I failed English, I have to do summer school and hang out here. Believe me, I would *never* have asked for a library card if it had been me in front of that judge –"

Paul stopped, realizing what he had just said, and he began to backtrack. Blushing, his words raced on.

"The only reason my mom told me was because I kept bugging her about you, and I knew she was hiding something. I was just kind of curious about why you were hanging out here all the time. And why you acted so weird that day in the alley.

"So I suppose she told you that my mom's in jail, too, right?"

Paul looked at Mel, then he looked down at the carpet, and then back at her. "No, actually, she didn't."

In the moment, his reply only made things worse. And Mel couldn't believe that she'd even said it. She hated the thought of Paul and his mom talking about her, and about Cecily.

"Yeah, well, it's true. And the guy in the alley – he walked like my mom's creepy ex-boyfriend, okay? Now do you know enough?"

"Hey, man, I'm sorry. It's not why I asked," Paul said. "It wasn't that at all." Then, changing the subject, he asked, "Do you want to play a game of chess?"

"No, I've got to go," Mel said.

"Well, do you want to hang out tomorrow?" Paul asked.

"No, I can't."

"Okay, how about Tuesday?"

"I can't."

"All right. Wednesday," Paul said. He said it as though he was going to keep asking until Mel agreed.

She felt herself almost laugh and cry as she looked into the comical expression on Paul's face. "Well, it depends," she said.

"Depends on what?"

Mel didn't know what to say. "I guess it depends on what you want to do."

"How does going for a bike ride sound?"

"I don't have one."

"We've got two," Paul said. "I could bring them by your place."

"Okay, maybe." A smile crept onto Mel's face.

"So are you still all, like, super busy-busy until Wednesday?" Paul asked. And then he laughed.

"No, I guess not."

"I'll go back to my first question, then. Do you want to hang out tomorrow?"

"I guess so," Mel said.

Until now, Mel hadn't noticed that their entire

conversation had been carried out in the foyer of the library. But she was glad Paul had persevered; he had in some way proven that he wasn't just feeling sorry for her – he actually wanted to be her friend.

"Paul," Marilyn said, "I'm heading out. Are you ready to go?"

Paul looked at his mom as she approached, then at Mel. "So, we're on?" he asked, shifting his head and shoulders from side to side and smiling.

"Sure. What time?"

"I'll be there at eleven."

"Okay, but I should probably tell you where I live."

"Oh, yeah, right." Paul was blushing, and Mel wanted to laugh.

 I live near Frohberger's on Maple," she told him.

"Frohberger's, on Maple, at eleven, I'll be there," Paul said.

"Great, I'll meet you at the bus stop," Mel answered and then watched as Paul left the library with his mom; she felt a pang of envy.

Mel renewed two of her books and then left the library. The sun was shining. She decided to walk. It gave her time to think about Paul, the alley, and Paul saying that she was his only friend – at least in Riverview. She thought about seeing him tomorrow, and about wanting to know him better. She replayed their conversation over in her mind as she walked; she didn't think about Craig. It seemed like only minutes had passed and she was at Frohberger's corner.

27

Morning Mountain

Mel sat on the bench at the bus stop, waiting for Paul. In some ways, it was hard to believe that the days, which had passed so slowly in the beginning, were now going more quickly. *Only nine days remained until Cecily returned.*

"I can't believe you brought two bikes on a bus," she said as she watched Paul unload them from the bike rack on the front of bus.

Paul handed her the smaller bike. "So," he said, getting on his bike, "are you up for a bit of a climb?"

"Sure," Mel answered.

They biked to the outskirts of town, to a trailhead marked Morning Mountain Trail.

"We're going to ride up here for about forty-five minutes to an hour," Paul said.

"We're going to climb up a *mountain*, on bikes, for an hour?"

"Yeah, but believe me, it's worth it," Paul said.

"Okay," Mel said, even though she doubted she'd be able to do it. "I'll let you go first."

For over an hour, they pedaled uphill. Mel's legs ached, her lungs were tight, and her mouth was dry. More than once she got off her bike and tried walking, but it wasn't much easier. About the time she figured she would just turn her bike around and go back down, Paul called out from up ahead that they were almost there. She drew on the little energy she had left in her legs, and pedaled up the trail.

It took a moment for Mel to catch her breath, but once she was able to take in her surroundings, she could see that what Paul had said was true. The view was amazing; you could see the entire city, as well as the river as it flowed out into the valley. Mel added this spot to her list of beautiful places.

They got off their bikes and sat in the grass. Mel watched the clouds float through the cerulean blue sky. In all the places she and Cecily had been, Mel couldn't remember ever being on top of a mountain. Of course, it wasn't a *real* mountain, like the ones in the Rockies, but it was as close to a mountain as she'd ever been. Mel had had never felt more alive, but she quickly corrected herself: it wasn't more *alive* that she was feeling, it was a feeling of being *normal*. She glanced over at Paul; he was lying in the grass and sipping from his water bottle. He looked back in her direction, but inadvertently let the water from the bottle pour onto his face. Mel laughed uncontrollably. Paul shook the remaining water in her direction, which only made her laugh harder. Paul jumped up, pushed her back into the grass and sat on her stomach, using his hands to hold her hands down.

"So, you still think it's funny?"

"Yes," Mel choked out as she kept laughing.

Letting one of her hands go, he grabbed a stalk of dried grass and put the stem end into his mouth. "You still think it's funny?" he asked, tickling her nose with the grassy tip and grabbing hold of her hand again.

"Yes!" Mel yelled back.

"Still?" Paul wiggled the grass tip against her eyes.

Mel was almost unable to speak. She was no longer laughing at the sight of Paul dumping his water on his face, or because he was tickling her. She was laughing purely because it felt so good to laugh.

"Okay," Paul said as he let her hands go. "You win, but I'll bet I can beat you to the bottom."

"No doubt," Mel said. She was still finding it difficult to contain her laughter. "I just hope I don't get killed weaving down through all the trees."

"You'll be fine; just don't use your front brake –

whatever you do. We can be down in fifteen."

"Fifteen minutes? It took us an hour to get up here."

"Yeah," Paul said as he started to pedal away. "Fifteen minutes. Bet you can't beat me to the bottom."

Paul was soon out of sight, but it didn't matter. The ride down was better than Mel could have imagined. The air was cool on her face, the trail was fast, and she was free – the way you feel after an honest bout of laugher. Other than the odd tree branch swiping her across her chest or legs, the ride down was uneventful. Paul was waiting for her at the trailhead.

"So, what do you think? Was the ride worth the climb?"

"Definitely," Mel said, getting off her bike. Her legs were wobbly, not so much from fear as from the exhilaration of pushing her feet into the pedals for fifteen minutes.

They walked the bikes back to Frohberger's.

"Who's your friend?" Mr. Frohberger asked Mel when he saw them parking their bikes in the rack.

"My name is Paul."

"Ed Frohberger," Mr. Frohberger said as he reached out his hand to Paul. Then he turned to Mel. "I've decided to start carrying ice cream again. The old cooler finally gave up the ghost, and the dealer managed to sell me a real honker, works like a charm. Come in and take a look. It's brand-spanking new."

Mel and Paul followed Mr. Frohberger into the store and looked in the cooler. There were two flavors.

"You two are my first customers, so the ice cream is on the house. What would you like, strawberry or chocolate, or a little of each?"

Mel chose strawberry, and Paul opted for a half and half. The scoops were huge. They sat down on the front steps, enjoying their cones and each other's company. Mr. Frohberger waited until they both voiced their approval of the ice cream and then went back inside, leaving them to talk about the climb, laugh about the water, and enjoy the sun.

When Paul's bus approached, they both noticed it stopping, but neither of them mentioned it. Mel waited with Paul until the next bus arrived, and helped him put the bikes on the bus rack. Walking back to Gladys's from Frohberger's, she started a list of everything that happened that day. It was all good.

28

The Third Saturday

Mel counted the days.

Tuesday had been nine days, Wednesday seven. Thursday six, Friday five, and now it was already Saturday again. Paul had come by the library every day, and it seemed that he came specifically to see her, often taking the bus with her to Frohberger's, then the two of them getting a pop or an ice cream while they waited for Paul's bus.

Mel found herself feeling guilty that the days until Cecily's return seemed to rush by, almost too quickly. She began rehearsing what she would tell Cecily – hoping she could convince her that staying, at least until the end of the summer, was a good idea. And she felt guilty for not sending another letter – even though she'd often thought about writing Cecily and telling her about the job or Paul or even about how Gladys had seemed better, not so angry all the time. But now, with only four days left, a letter wouldn't arrive in time. *And anyway*, Mel decided, *it would be easier to convince Cecily to stay if she saw for herself how good things were.*

Mel was perched on the little red chair in the library. Since that first day, she'd become much more comfortable in front of all the kids and parents. As she finished reading *Tikki Tikki Tembo*, she looked up and thought she saw Cecily, her face peering around the corner. But by the time the cluster of children and parents had left the carpet, Cecily – if she'd been there at all – was gone.

"I'm probably just seeing things," Mel whispered.

She walked through the library and out into the street and around the corner. No sign of Cecily. *It couldn't have been her; she wouldn't come and then go.*

Mel went back into the library, gathered up the books from the story circle, and picked up the floor cushions, stacking them one on top of another in her arms. She walked back to the window and was flooded with memories of Cecily reading to her, of being tired and curling up in Cecily's thick coat while she read *Goodnight Moon* or *Guess How Much I Love You*. Mel remembered the feeling of drifting into contented sleep. But that was a long time ago, and there had been a lot of libraries in her life since then.

It surprised Mel when Lisa came up behind her. "Everything okay?" she asked.

"Was there a woman with long braids standing by the display over there?" Mel asked.

"Not that I saw," Lisa said, "but I was listening to you. You did a fantastic job!"

"Thanks," Mel said as she shrugged her shoulders. "It was fun."

29

Three Days

The next three days came and went. Mel knew that by now Cecily should have come for her. She went to the calendar in the kitchen to recount the days.

Gladys came in, pulled a hot plate of food out of the oven, and set it on the table.

"Your mother dropped off a letter," she said once Mel started eating. "You can read it when you're finished."

Gladys placed the letter on the table, next to the keys that had been there for almost a month. Everything about Gladys's voice told Mel the same thing: the letter was bringing bad news.

Each small bite stuck in Mel's throat. If Cecily had found a place for them to live, she'd be here. She'd have at least called. She wouldn't leave a letter. Getting up, Mel filled the chipped enamel sink halfway with warm water, washed the dishes, dried them, and put them away. She didn't rush. Cecily had been gone either thirty-two days or thirty-five; it depended on how you counted.

Even without reading the letter, Mel knew what it was about.

Mel picked it up and walked to the couch.

My Dearest Mel,

The words poured off the page, and Mel could feel them drowning her. Everything had been good, too good. And now it was all crumbling.

I know this will make you sad, but right now I can't be there for you.

Cecily wasn't coming for her. It was probably the drugs, the booze, the pressure of needing to find a place to live. She'd given up. She hadn't even started, and she was already giving up. It was all the things Mel never let herself say, but had always known.

You're better off with Gladys. You have a home, a job. Gladys says you've got friends. I just need some time.

Gladys turned the volume on the TV down, and made herself a cup of tea. Mel kept reading.

There are some things I need to work out. I'm sorry, Mel. I love you, like the flowers need the rain, I love you. I love you, I love you, I love you.

Mel buried her face into the satin pillow, damming the tears that flowed down her cheeks, and she crumpled the damp sheet of paper in her fist. Her muffled sobs masked the sound of Gladys's pacing back and forth from the table in the kitchen to the living room doorway.

30

The Locked Room

When Mel woke up the next morning, she was warm, and she found a second blanket on top of the crocheted one she normally slept under. She could hear Gladys in the kitchen. Mel got up, smoothed the crumpled letter she'd hung on to all night, folded the blankets, and walked into the kitchen on her way to the bathroom. The TV was off and she braced herself for what Gladys might say.

"Wasn't my idea for her to go running off again." Gladys paused, and Mel sensed that Gladys might actually be making room for her to say something, but Mel chose not to. Instead, she tucked the letter into her pocket.

"First she takes you in the middle of the night, doesn't even say good-bye." Gladys's voice started to break up, and her eyes started to tear. "Tux was too sick to be gallivanting all over the country looking for you."

Mel didn't wait for Gladys to finish; she walked into the bathroom and closed the door. She looked at her reflection in the mirror. Her eyes were swollen from last night's tears, but today her resolve had hardened: she would find Cecily.

"You can have the side room," Gladys said as Mel walked back into the kitchen. There was a sense of urgency in Gladys's voice, as though she wanted to settle on a decision regarding where Mel would stay – and she wanted to settle it now.

Gladys stood and walked over to the small enamel cupboard. She pulled first on one corner, then the other, walking it forward and away from the door. She unlatched the slide lock, opened the door, and turned on the light. For weeks, Mel had wondered what was behind that door, but today it didn't matter.

For the most part, the room was empty. There was the frame of a wrought iron bed, an old dresser with a cracked mirror, and a piece of painted vinyl on the floor that was meant to look like carpet. A painted high chair sat in the corner. There was also a large steamer trunk.

"You can use the cushions off the couch until we get you a mattress. The trunk will have to stay for now . . . might be some things in there we could sell to get you some new sheets and a proper blanket."

Mel glanced at Gladys's angular frame standing just off to the side of the narrow doorway.

"I don't need the side room," Mel said defiantly. "I'm going to find Cecily."

Mel turned, walked into the living room, gathered her library books, and stuffed the rest of her things into her backpack.

As she walked past the kitchen doorway to the apartment door, she caught a glimpse of Gladys. She was sweeping up bread crumbs.

"There's no point looking for her," Gladys said without looking up. "That's what Cecily does – she disappears."

Mel ignored Gladys's words, and left.

Once outside, she looked down the street at Frohberger's sign and decided to walk along Thirty-Seventh and back up Thirty-Ninth instead, and avoid the store altogether.

Now more than ever, she needed to conserve the little money she had left. On the way downtown, she dropped her books off at the library. She didn't expect to run into Paul, but there he was. He appeared to be waiting for a man to finish talking with his mom. Mel figured it might be his dad.

Mel didn't know what to say to Paul. For sure she wasn't going to tell him about the letter or why Cecily had been in jail or about the shoplifting or the booze or the drugs. She wasn't going to tell him about waiting outside in the cold for shelters to reopen, only to find out that they didn't have any room. She wasn't going to tell him about traveling from place to place and never belonging anywhere. She wasn't going to tell him about eating in soup kitchens or about all the stupid lists that she and Cecily made. She knew that she wouldn't tell him about Rose finding her under the overpass, or about begging for money, or about the judge telling her that she was important. She knew she would not tell him that he was her first real friend. She wasn't going to tell him how great it felt to laugh with him. She wasn't going to tell him about any one of those things. And so when Paul spotted her and ran over and asked if she was okay, Mel lied. But just looking at him, she saw he knew the truth.

"I've got to go," she said.

"What's happening?"

"I've got to go," Mel repeated.

"I'll come with you," Paul said as he gave a quick glance in the direction of his mom and the man on the other side of the counter.

"No, I'll see you later," Mel told him.

In fact, she didn't actually know when or if she would see him again. She turned and left the library. If anyone knew where Cecily was, it would be Rose. Mel continued on down the street to the soup kitchen. As she walked, she made a mental list of all the places Cecily had told her about on the first night. Places to bask in the sun, or sing for cash, or hang out with friends. She planned to go by them all.

She looked into the face of every person she saw on the street, hoping to find someone who would tell her they'd seen Cecily just up that way, just over there, just a few minutes ago. But what she really feared was that Cecily was lying in an alley somewhere, next to a dumpster, cold and alone.

As Mel opened the back door to the soup kitchen, she pulled the letter from her pocket. Rose was preparing lunch. Fearless immediately found her. She lifted him into her arms and he began to purr. Mel could tell by the look on Rose's face that Rose knew why she'd come.

"She's not here," Rose said, hardly looking up.

"But she was, wasn't she?" Mel stood there, stroking Fearless's head and back.

"You've got a roof over your head; you've got food on the table and a warm place to sleep. The streets are no place for a kid," Rose said as she continued chopping carrots into little discs.

Tears began streaming down Mel's face. "So is she coming back?"

Rose stopped what she was doing. Gus, who was

standing nearby, continued chopping, but said nothing.

Mel set Fearless back down on the kitchen floor and walked toward the back door.

Rose laid the knife on the counter. "She's giving you the only chance you've got at a decent life," Rose said.

"What do you mean 'a decent life'?" Mel shouted. "She left me with an angry old woman who hates me! You call that a decent life? You told me everything was going to be okay. Do you remember that?"

Rose walked over to the closet by the back door, retrieved her purse, and brought out a black-and-white strip of photographs of Mel and Cecily.

"Cecily asked me to give this to you," Rose said as she handed Mel the print.

Mel remembered it from the photo booth in the mall the summer before. "She's not coming back, is she?"

"I don't know," Rose said, looking Mel straight in the face.

"I'm going to find her."

"Now, just hold on a minute," Rose called out. "I'm coming with you. We'll take the van."

Mel stood next to the van while Rose unlocked the doors, and then they climbed in. Fearless meowed at the van door. Rose picked him up and set him on Mel's lap.

They drove down every alley and every street in

the downtown. They went to the campsite Cecily had talked about on the first night in Riverview and by the overpass. Mel got out and called Cecily's name. She was nowhere.

"So tell me," Rose asked, ending the silence as they drove back into town, "did you get the job at the library?"

"Yeah," Mel answered.

"What do you do?"

"I just read stories to kids."

"Do you like it?"

"I did."

"What's the best part?"

"I thought she'd come back," Mel said, unable to make small talk.

"This isn't necessarily forever. It's just for now. It's what is best for now," Rose said.

"Did she tell you she'd come back for me?"

"She just told me she was doing what was best for you. I know it isn't any of my business, but I think she's right."

After a few minutes, Rose spoke again.

"Fearless and I will drive you back to your grandmother's."

"I already told her that I didn't need the room," Mel said.

She cradled Fearless in her arms. Rose continued to drive. Neither of them said anything until they reached the corner of Thirty-Seventh and Maple; Rose pulled the van into a parking spot.

"Do you want me to go in with you?" Rose asked.

"No, I can go by myself." Mel opened the door, got out, and set Fearless on the van seat.

"There's something else," Rose began, "something I want to ask you."

"What's that?" Mel asked. She gave Fearless another pet.

"Do you think your grandmother would let you keep him?"

"Never," Mel said half laughing. "She hates – everything."

"Well, if you'd like to give it a try and ask her, I'll wait down here," Rose said. "You go in and ask her. If she says no, come back out and I'll take him with me. I'll give you twenty minutes, and if I don't see you, I'll know everything worked out."

"She'll say no. I know it."

"She might, but if you don't ask, you'll never know. And the truth is: he needs a home."

Mel could feel her jaw shaking and it made it hard to speak. She picked Fearless up and began walking toward the apartment building door; her heart was pounding. Just before she went in, she looked back. Rose was there, standing by the old VW, and waving for her to keep going. Mel climbed the stairs, working the words and thoughts and her plans around in her head. Gladys met her at the door.

"What's that you've got there – a dead cat?"

Mel held Fearless tight. "He needs a home," Mel said as she tried to swallow the enormous lump that kept rising up from her heart and into her throat. Tears rolled down her face. "Actually, we both do."

Gladys looked at Mel, and then at Fearless, who was staring at her as though he was reading her mind.

"Well . . . I guess if you're a matched set, we'll have to let him stay," Gladys said as she closed the door behind them.

Fearless wiggled around in Mel's arms until she put him down on the floor. He tiptoed on the cool linoleum; it was as though he was afraid that his paws would stick if he left them down for too long. He cautiously checked out every corner of the apartment.

Gladys paid no attention to him as she went to the stove. She poured the hot water from the kettle into the Brown Betty teapot and pulled a woolen tea cozy over top. She reached into the cupboard and brought down two cups that hung from small brass hooks. Once the tea had steeped, she filled the cups. Then, picking up the can of Red Label, she poured a little into a saucer and set it on the floor, and the remaining milk she poured into Mel's cup. The evaporated milk was thick, and Mel watched as it swirled into her tea, changing it from a dark, deep red to a warm, creamy brown. They didn't talk about the letter. They didn't talk about Cecily, or about Mel leaving or staying, or about the future. They just sat and drank tea, and when they were finished, Mel got ready for bed, went back to the couch, and slept.

31

First Light

In the morning, Mel woke up to find Fearless cuddled up beside her and Gladys peeling the tinfoil off the windows. Some of the tinfoil, from around the window near the stove, needed to be scraped off with a knife, as it had been stuck to the window for so many years. It was coming off in tiny slivers.

"Well, don't just sit there looking like you've never seen the light of day."

Mel noticed the tone in Gladys's voice. Gladys was trying to be funny.

"You can help me if you want," Gladys added.

Mel wasn't sure if they were just *changing* the tinfoil, or if they were taking it down for good. *But so what*, she decided, *let's just get the tinfoil off for however long and let the sun in.*

"There," Gladys said when they were done. "That looks better."

Then Gladys went to her bedroom and came back

with a pair of folded cotton curtains. She handed Mel the rod and asked her to feed the curtains onto it.

"They're nice," Mel said, although they smelled heavily of mothballs.

Fearless didn't appear to be bothered by the smell, and instead found himself a spot on the windowsill behind the curtain.

"You know, if we wedged a little knife in between the sill and the window, we might be able to get the windows to open," Mel suggested.

"Oh, don't go getting all carried away," Gladys said, sitting to rest in her chair. "There are no locks on any of these windows. I painted them shut years ago as a means of keeping out thieves."

A smile crept onto Gladys's face, as though she realized that what she had just said was a wee bit silly. She stood up, opened the cutlery drawer, and handed Mel a butter knife. "I'm not sure this will do it, but you can give it a try."

While Mel worked to pry the window open, Gladys fixed them both some peanut butter and honey sandwiches. Mel could feel Gladys watching her. Once Mel was finished, they sat down at the table.

"Listen," Mel said to herself more than to anyone else. "You can hear the birds sing."

Gladys opened a can of Red Label milk and poured some into her teacup. Then, after a sip of tea, she looked up. "Both of these keys are for you."

Mel glanced at the keys.

"I should have given them to you in the first place. I just . . . I just thought . . . ," Gladys started.

Mel finished her sentence. "You thought I'd steal your things."

"I was wrong, and I'm sorry." Gladys said and then gently slid the keys in Mel's direction.

Mel picked them up and put them in her pocket. Her thought was to attach them to the key chain that also held the Pinto car key, which she'd kept safe zipped in the front pocket of her pack all this time.

32

The Last Show

Mr. Frohberger was sweeping the front steps when she walked by.

"Who's that you have slung around your neck?"

"This is Fearless."

"Well, how about that. Welcome to the neighborhood, Fearless," Mr. Frohberger said, rubbing Fearless's neck and head.

Mel wondered if Gladys had told Mr. Frohberger about Cecily, and the letter.

"So, where are you off to today, Mel?"

"Oh, I'm just taking Fearless out for walk."

"Well, if he gets tired of walking, which I doubt he will, sitting up there like some kind of prince, you can bring him back here and see if he can track down a mouse or two. I don't know why, but about this time of year, every rodent for forty miles tries to make a home in the store."

"I'll do that," Mel said, stroking Fearless's head.

"Stop in on your way back, anyway. I found something I think you might like to have."

Mel and Fearless walked for most of the day. They went by the park and the office buildings near the central bus stop, and they dropped by the soup kitchen; Cecily was nowhere to be found.

Mel didn't feel much like talking when she got back to Frohberger's, but she had said she would stop and so she did.

"Here you go," Mr. Frohberger said, sliding a piece of paper out from between two pieces of cardboard. "It's the poster I printed up for your grandfather's last show." Fearless leaped from Mel's shoulder to the counter.

Mel examined the dark black letters done in calligraphy, and the pen-and-ink sketch of Tux: his smile, his black tuxedo, top hat, and the swirl of imagined magic spiraling around him.

"He would have wanted you to have it," Mr. Frohberger said as he stroked Fearless.

Mel stared at that poster. "Did he really look like that?"

"More or less. He wore a tuxedo and top hat – well, only when he was performing and all, but he always wore that smile. You've got his eyes."

Mel slid the poster back between the pieces of cardboard and looked up at Mr. Frohberger.

"Thank you," she said, and then she turned and began to walk out the door.

"Oh! Don't forget this guy!"

"Come on, Fearless," Mel called. "And thanks again, Mr. Frohberger. This is great."

As Mel opened the door, Fearless scampered out onto the sidewalk and across the road.

33

Dancing in Silver

The apartment smelled of sausages and eggs cooking, and
Fearless headed straight for the kitchen when they came
through the door. Mel followed him.

"What's that you have there?" Gladys asked.

"A poster. Mr. Frohberger gave it to me."

"Is it a poster of Tux?"

"It is. Do you want to see it?" Mel carefully pulled
the poster from between the cardboard and laid it on the
table.

Gladys sat looking at the picture, her breathing deep-
ening and slowing, and then she began to speak, more to
herself than to Mel. Words flowed from her lips – only
the occasional word loud enough for Mel to make out.
Even so, Gladys's voice seemed rhythmic, punctuated by
moments of silence as though she was listening for a reply.
Mel heard her name, "Melody," included in the strands
of words beaded together. And although she couldn't fully
hear the words, she understood the meaning, and she

could tell that what Mr. Frohberger had said was true: Gladys loved Tux.

After awhile, Gladys stood and went to Cecily's old bedroom. She dragged the dark wooden steamer trunk into the kitchen. Mel expected the trunk to be full of things like pillows, old clothes, or other uninteresting things often stored in mothballs. She couldn't have been more wrong. The first thing Gladys lifted out of the trunk was a framed newspaper article picturing a man in a swallowtailed black tuxedo and top hat with a white stick.

"The Terrific Tux Tulley" the headline read.

Gladys wiped the dust off the frame with the edge of her skirt, and stood the framed picture on the table.

Mel stared at the contents of the trunk: silk handkerchiefs – four or five different colors – boxes, calipers, rulers, mirrors, a folded three-legged table, files full of papers, and a hinged box. In a space all of its own, and carefully folded and wrapped in tissue, was Tux's suit. Beside the suit sat a hatbox.

"Magic isn't something you buy in a store," Gladys said, her hands brushing the surface of the satin hatbox as she sat down.

Mel looked at Gladys, at the slightly pink color in her face.

"Tux used to say that everyone needs a little magic in their lives; it gives them hope."

Hope. The word seemed odd, Mel thought, *coming from Gladys's mouth, but in a way it seemed right.*

"And when Cecily left, taking you with her, it broke his heart, broke both our hearts." Gladys paused, took in a breath, and then continued. "Tux looked day and night. He and Ed Frohberger, they looked for weeks, even got in Ed's old Impala and drove to the city. When everyone else had given up hope, Ed Frohberger kept going out with Tux. More than just about anything, your Grandpa Tux loved you. Nothing would make him happier than to know that you're home and that you're safe."

Gladys reached into the trunk and picked up a small photo album, the kind with black paper pages and gold foil tabs holding in the photographs.

"These, here, are Tux's parents. I never met them; they stayed in the old country. This here," Gladys ran her finger along the line of children, stopping at the smallest, "this is Tux. He was three years old." About the age you were when he last saw you."

Gladys turned the page. There was another photograph of Tux; only the name Theodore was written below it. He was fourteen years old. Mel smiled as she looked up at Gladys and then back down at the album.

Gladys turned page after page, each time telling the story of each person preserved in the black-and-white photos. Mel noticed there were no photographs of Gladys's family, no photos of Cecily. What Mel had hoped for as the pages turned was that there would be pictures of her, as a baby, from those first three years when she had lived at least part of the time with Gladys and Tux, here. But as Gladys turned the last page, Mel accepted that there wouldn't be. Gladys reached for the trunk lid and closed it.

"Not much we can sell in here," she said.

Moments later, Gladys got up from the table and went into her room, returning with a small album and another photograph suspended in a simple silver frame. She handed the photograph to Mel. It was Tux, and he was holding a little girl. They were twirling, the girl's natural ringlets swirling across her face. Her mouth was open and she was laughing. Mel closed her eyes, and not only could she feel herself spinning, she could also hear Mr. Frohberger whistling, and she and Tux were dancing. They were on the sidewalk just outside the store. And deep in that place that was hurting, she knew it was a memory – not a want-to-have, pretend-to have, try-to-have memory, but a real memory.

"That picture," Gladys said when Mel opened her eyes, "belongs to you."

Gladys's fingers gently stroked the small satin album. Mel wondered if Gladys was going to cry.

"And this album is for you, too."

Mel picked up the album from Gladys's hands. Her fingers traced the embossed italic gold letters: C-E-C-I-L-Y.

"I really miss her," Mel said, looking up at Gladys.

"I know you do," Gladys said as she reached out and touched Mel's hand.

34
Good-bye to Paul

The last week Paul was in Riverview, he and Mel spent every day together. They played chess in the library, walked along the river, and ate ice cream on the steps of Frohberger's. And then on one especially clear day, they rode the bikes back up the mountain. Mel told Paul about her list of beautiful places, and they agreed that Morning Mountain belonged on the list. They talked about their lives, where they had been, and what they had seen; some of it was funny and some of it was sad. Paul told Mel about his parents and about the divorce. Mel told Paul about the letter and Rose and the four-pose picture of her with Cecily, and she told him that Cecily had left. She was surprised how good it felt just to tell the whole truth, just this once, to someone who could actually hear it.

On the last night Paul was in town, his mom invited Mel over for dinner. They ate pizza and watched a movie, and when it was over, Paul and his mom drove her back home.

As Mel opened the van door, Paul also opened the door on his side.

"I can walk myself in," Mel said quickly.

"I'll be right back," Paul said to his mom, ignoring Mel's comment.

"See you at the library," Marilyn said as she turned and smiled at Mel.

"Yeah, for sure. And thanks for the pizza and for the ride home."

Neither Paul nor Mel spoke as they walked to the apartment building. Mel wondered if Paul was also listening to his own thoughts, sorting out what to say. In her head, thoughts came, left, and returned, but she said nothing as they climbed the stairs.

Mel unlocked the door to the apartment to find Gladys sitting on the couch with her hands in her lap.

"Paul," Mel said, looking at Paul and then to Gladys, "this is my grandma." Gladys smiled, first at Mel, and then at Paul.

"Nice to meet you," Paul said.

"It's nice to meet you, too," Gladys answered.

Fearless rubbed himself against Mel's leg and slipped out the open door and down the stairs.

"Uh, I need to let Fearless out the bottom door," Mel said as much to Paul as to Gladys. She was grateful for the excuse to walk Paul back down to the entry. They both stopped when they reached the sidewalk.

Paul glanced over his shoulder at the waiting van, and then up to Gladys's apartment window. He took in a deep breath, pushed his hands into the pockets of his faded jean jacket, and brought his eyes back to Mel.

"So, I'll be back to visit my mom at Thanksgiving. Do you think you'll be here?"

Mel smiled. "Yeah, I'm not planning on going anywhere."

"Great – I'll call you."

"I'd like that," Mel said.

Paul turned and walked back to the van, and Mel walked back up the stairs to Gladys's.

35

The Fourth Saturday

Mel finished her storytime shift at the library and was walking toward the soup kitchen when she saw her.

"Cecily!" Mel yelled as she began running.

Cecily turned. Mel slowed to a jog.

"Cecily?" Mel said, this time making sure it was, in fact, her mom.

"Oh God, Mel," Cecily said. "I'm so sorry."

Cecily wrapped her arms around Mel's shoulders. Mel couldn't imagine anything feeling better.

"I didn't know what to do," Cecily said. "It just seemed like the best thing to do, you at Gladys's, having friends, a job, and . . ."

"It's okay; I knew you'd come back," Mel told her. "I knew you wouldn't just leave me."

"I got here today and I was hoping that you'd come back with me. I just called Gladys." Then she paused and added, "We came to get the car out of the city pound and we were going to go by the library next." Cecily leaned down and kissed the top of Mel's head.

"We?" Mel asked as she pulled away and looked up at Cecily.

Cecily's eyes shifted to the road.

Mel followed them. It was the Pinto. And in the car was Craig.

"Craig?" Mel asked, looking back at Cecily. Her heart started to hammer against her chest.

"Hey, Mel," Craig said over the bass music, leaning toward the passenger seat. "Are you coming with us?"

Mel didn't answer. Instead her eyes went back to Cecily, then to the sidewalk, and then away. "What did he say about us taking the car? Did he say anything about my journal and . . ." Her voice trailed off.

"It's going to be okay," Cecily said, reading Mel's thoughts. "God, I missed you so much."

"I missed you too, but Craig . . ." He was the last person Mel wanted to see again.

"Don't worry. Things are going to be different this time," Cecily assured her. "I promise."

"But you said there was no going back."

"Sometimes plans change," Cecily whispered.

"I have a cat." Mel said the words as a matter of fact, making sure it was clear to Cecily that Fearless was coming with her.

"Okay," Cecily said, and then looked down at Craig. "A cat's okay, don't you think, Craig?"

"Yeah, no problem," Craig said, nodding his head.

Cecily opened the front door. Mel hesitated but then opened the door to the back and got in, her eyes on the soup kitchen door as they pulled away from the curb. Mel would have liked to have gone in, to have said good-bye to Rose and Gus.

"Gladys said she'd pack up your things for you," Cecily said as she looked over her shoulder at Mel.

Mel nodded but said nothing.

It seemed like Craig was looking in the rearview mirror every few seconds, making eye contact. Mel decided to keep her head down. As they went past Frohberger's, she looked sideways into the shop window, hoping to catch a glimpse of Mr. Frohberger.

Craig pulled the car up to the curb in front of Gladys's.

"Make it quick," he told Mel.

"Yeah, I will."

"Are you going to come in with me?" Mel whispered to Cecily through the window of the car door.

"No, that's probably not a good idea," Cecily said, looking at Craig and then at the apartment.

"Maybe you could stay here, with me and Gladys.

She seems different – nicer," Mel whispered in an even softer voice.

"Just go get your things, okay?" Cecily whispered back.

Mel turned and walked toward the front door of the apartment building. She didn't exactly know why, but when she reached the door to Gladys's apartment, she knocked. Maybe it was a case of nerves, or maybe it was because it gave her a few extra moments to think about what she was going to say.

Gladys opened the door. Mel looked straight into her eyes.

"Can Cecily stay here – with us?"

"I gave her that option, when she came by and dropped off the letter," Gladys said.

"You did?" Mel asked.

"At the time, I didn't know if it was better to tell you or not."

Without really thinking it through, Mel ran back down the stairs to the idling Pinto.

"Gladys said you can stay," she told Cecily, not giving away that she understood Cecily already knew that.

"Go get your things," Cecily answered back.

Craig revved the engine. "Come on, Mel, we don't have all day."

"You don't have to go with him," Mel said. Her voice

was tense, and she was on the verge of yelling the words at Cecily.

"Look," Cecily said, "just go back and get the cat and your things."

"I just thought maybe . . ."

"Go. Now!" Cecily said harshly, and then she lifted her menthol cigarette to her mouth and inhaled.

Mel ran.

Gladys was waiting with a bag of Mel's clothes in one arm and Fearless in the other when Mel opened the door.

"She said I could bring Fearless," Mel said, looking at Gladys's sad face.

"I know," Gladys said. Her voice was quiet.

The *beep! beep!* from the horn on the Pinto came through the open window in the kitchen.

"I'm sorry," Mel said as she lifted both Fearless and her things from Gladys's arms. "Really, I am."

"Me too," Gladys said. Her lower jaw was shaking.

The honking sounded again, only now the beeps were longer and felt louder.

"I promise I'll visit – I'll come for Thanksgiving."

Gladys nodded.

"Tell Mr. Frohberger – tell him – I'll see him then, too."

Gladys kept nodding.

The horn gave a long blare.

"And call Lisa at the library. Tell her I'm really sorry."

"I will," Gladys said as she took in a deep breath.

Mel ran down the stairs, out the door, and along the sidewalk. Just as she was about to get in the car she looked up at the kitchen window. Gladys was there.

Mel paused for a brief moment. She lifted her hand from her bag of clothes, gave a little wave, and got into the car.

As they pulled away from the curb, Craig looked into the rearview mirror at her. "I was hoping that you'd come back with us," he said with a continued stare. And then there was a short pause. "And just so you know, your books are all safe and sound."

A shiver ran up Mel's spine. Her heart began to pound and she knew he'd found her journal. Mel knew she needed to say she was sorry, get it over with, tell him that that stuff about wanting to call the police was a lie. But the words sat, as though they had a will of their own and were unwilling to be spoken. As Craig shifted gears and sped up, a bottle, half full, rolled from under the driver's seat to the space at her feet, and then it rolled back under the front seat again. Mel recognized the bottle and its contents. Whiskey.

36

Home

"Stop!" Mel yelled.

Craig was caught off guard and he screeched the car to a halt. Mel swung the door open and jumped out, taking her things and Fearless with her.

"What are you doing?" Cecily asked, half asking, half yelling.

"I'm going home," Mel said as she stepped away from the car. "Are you coming with me?"

Craig revved the engine.

"Please, Mel, don't do this," Cecily pleaded.

"Are you?" Mel asked the question again even though she knew the answer.

"I'm sorry, Mel, I can't. Not right now." Cecily shook her head. "I'm really sorry."

"Me too," Mel said.

Cecily closed her eyes, and Mel watched as tears streamed down Cecily's cheeks.

"White light," Mel whispered as the smoke from

Cecily's cigarette drifted from the car out the window.

Cecily nodded.

Craig hit the gas pedal hard, and they were gone.

Epilogue

Mel used some of the money she earned at the library to buy a new pair of jeans and a shirt; the rest she tucked into a sock in the top drawer of her dresser, the one that used to be Cecily's. Gladys gave her money for a book bag and shoes.

On September 7, Mel walked down the school hallway to Room 214. She took a seat near the front, next to the window, and absorbed the laughter and excitement of her classmates recounting their summer adventures. Picking up the booklet that had been placed on her desk, she carefully folded back the cover and read the only words printed on the first page.

Magic is believing in yourself; if you can do that, you can make anything happen.

— Johann Wolfgang von Goethe,
German Playwright, Poet, Novelist, Dramatist

Mel smiled and thought about Cecily and Tux. If Cecily were here, she would have said it was a sign.